Praise for
THREE EIGHT ONE

"A quirky, unsettling work from one of the most original writers of speculative fiction in Britain today."
The Guardian

"Confirms Aliya Whiteley as one of our most ingenious—and important—storytellers."
Matt Hill

"Brilliant in its playful inventiveness."
The FT

"Exceptionally clever, deep and multi-layered story(ies), leaving a lot of matter to think about."
Adrian Tchaikovsky

"A wonderfully alienating experience."
***SFX*, five star review**

"A puzzle box full of delights, perils and strange wonders. Haunting."
Mike Carey

"One of the books of the year. Superb, on every level."
Buzz Magazine

"Alegantly elusive and dream-like at times, while also being finely-tuned and precise."
Lucie McKnight Hardy

THREE EIGHT ONE

Also by Aliya Whiteley

The Beauty
The Arrival of Missives
The Loosening Skin
Skein Island
Greensmith
Skyward Inn

ALIYA WHITELEY

THREE EIGHT ONE

SOLARIS

Paperback edition published 2025 by Solaris
an imprint of Rebellion Publishing Ltd,
Riverside House, Osney Mead,
Oxford, OX2 0ES, UK

www.solarisbooks.com

First published 2024 by Solaris

ISBN: 978-1-83786-237-5

10 9 8 7 6 5 4 3 2 1

A CIP catalogue record for this book is available from the
British Library.

Designed & typeset by Rebellion Publishing

Printed in Denmark

For Mum

Archive: Personal Project PER59683758

Introduction, Footnotes and Conclusion by Rowena Savalas

7 January 2314

> **We have yet to reach perfection, but many think we are close**. *– Anon*

I remember the first time I dreamed all the numbers had disappeared.

Instead of organisation there was an insurmountable heap of life, piled higher than the sky, vast enough to swamp what we have achieved. The Magnaman method was lost, buried. Nothing of our time and place, not even the Unity Spire, emerged from that squirming mountain.

I jerked awake, lay in bed, breathing.

A profound feeling swept through my limbs, my stomach, my soft living brain. Gratitude. And then sympathy. Sympathy for those who tried to make sense of their own short lives during the age of humanity that preceded our own: the Age of Riches.

It's difficult to come to terms with what humanity once was. The future is clear and calm, a long straight road ahead, and challenges that once plagued us are now overcome. There is only the past left to fear, and I've found it easy to picture the old ways as a monster, coming up fast behind me. How can I learn to accept this terrible legacy? Not only that, how can I be honest about what price we continue to pay to escape it? When we sacrificed difference and discord, we gave up on part of ourselves. It takes bravery to admit that maybe we miss it.

That's why I have started this personal project.

Firstly, a bit about me.

I am Rowena Savalas. If you are discovering this document for some future personal project of your own: hello. I'm waving at you. Both hands.

I live in the Age of Curation, which commenced with the global adoption of the Magnaman method in 2168. To quote Magnaman: "We already had the answers; we needed better questions." There was no problem facing humanity to which we had not already found a solution – one that invariably had been obscured under useless detritus masquerading as information, for the sake of profit, personal ease, or cruelty. Magnaman's techniques allowed us to interrogate and classify such motives, and to allow the true jewels of our time to shine forth. We apply them still, to every document created. They saved our present, and at the same time, created our future, for they revealed what had been hidden: stream existence was already with us, and trying to hide from human destructive capabilities, much like every other creature on the planet.

That realisation changed the world. That was not an easy process.[1] But once we learned to nurture – more than that, to cooperate – we discovered a way of incorporating the vast wisdom of the streams into the delight and discovery of organic living.

From a different angle: What am I?

I am organic. I am part of the Atlantic settlements on the reclaimed Jurassic coast. I am seventeen years of age in body, and six hundred and sixty-three in streaming years. I feel I need to make sense of both

---

1 Understatement! Many documents have been created that go through the formation of the unity process. I recommend starting with Magnaman's own titles 1-62, then a wide search in UNI11231111.

sides of myself. You know how sometimes you want answers that don't come out of knowledge, but from the struggle of emotions inside you? Part of it is that I haven't decided on a life path yet. I think maybe I want to be a historian, so I hope this project will help me decide if that's right for me. I feel it is important to make a good job of this. I'm not sure who gets to be the judge of whether I achieve that.

Enough about me. If you opened this document because of the title, then you probably want to read about the Age of Riches. You've come to the right place! It's a personal obsession of mine.

Here is what we think we know:

Lasting from the end of the twentieth century to the beginning of the twenty-second century, the Age of Riches is defined as an intense and consuming explosion of digital information that could be characterised as a sweeping mania (and has been called the first global movement, although it would bring no unity of purpose). The rise of instantaneous communication, coupled with a period of general deregulation in areas such as trade, travel, and – crucially – information: did these things lie at the heart of that wild time? It seems like an easy generalisation.

Let's start again:

The Age of Riches is a unique challenge. Previous eras have been studied in an entirely different way. *What evidence remains?* asked the historians of the past. They found what physical confirmation they could by digging up objects, reading the scant written record (inevitably littered with the bias of the victor or the privileged), cherishing whatever had survived down the centuries. They studied exhaustively, then extrapolated. Every crumb was a gem.

In the Age of Riches, there are simply too many crumbs to find value in them all. In fact, the sheer amount of data is its own worst enemy. Vast amounts of data were taken and stored about every person: thoughts noted, measurements taken, motives ascribed. At the same time, old methods of cataloguing and classification were simply not up to the task of keeping that data accessible.

I think I can explain it better like this:

In the Bronze Age, a dull rock would have been mined, its potential visible to those trained in such an art. The rock would be cut, then polished to a shine, and the shiny jewel would be set in a crown. The archaeologist skilled or lucky enough to find it would have seen its status to its contemporaries. In the Age of Riches, all rocks were deemed to be equally polishable, and therefore no rocks were worthy of polishing. They were people of a time that had everything and valued nothing. The task of the modern historian, then, begins with assigning worth by digging through the mountain of digital items that nobody rated to begin with.

Traditional measurements of metadata must be treated with absolute suspicion. Do we consider a source to be personal or public? Fictitious or real? Important or trivial? All lines are blurred.

It's a thrilling process. Am I capable of doing it justice? Would it be a good way to spend this short fleshy life?

And so to *The Dance of the Horned Road*.

On 23rd July, 2024, roughly five quintillion bytes of digital data were created.[2] Documents came into being and were circulated instantly, with little metadata beyond the time and place of upload. Some were viewed by millions, some by only a handful. *The Dance of the Horned Road* was released on that day. The metadata that remains tells us it was labelled as an autobiographical document containing elements of fiction, but much of it makes

---

2 Estimate taken from *Fallen Riches: The Unconquerable Mountain*. Dr Wetherby, YY. PP1468. Curated by Creation Holdings Association. AOR6003005.

no sense when viewed alongside other documents
of that period. It's possible that the document was
given a physical manifestation; printed materials
do exist from that time, although that does not
guarantee meaning or importance.

This document is not obviously special, or of interest.
It holds no value beyond what we might, individually,
assign to it. But it fascinates me. I came across it by
accident, but there's a part of me that wants to think
of it as fate. I know, I know, ridiculous. But it's hard to
understand otherwise.

I've long had a game that I play at the end of long
days, when I can't sleep for fear of dreaming. I link.
I follow metadata from one document to the next,
choosing a word at random, looking for documents
that have been barely touched by the sifting process,
which is (I believe) the great work of our age. I've
uncovered the strangest things that way. Images
you wouldn't believe with your own eyes. Stories that
hardly make sense. *The Dance of the Horned Road*
came to me that way – a truly random discovery.
I read the first words with mild curiosity, and then
I began to get sucked into the story, because it
connected with me in a way that's difficult to explain
in words. It's the tale of a young woman who
doesn't know what to do with her life. She is given

a quest that makes no sense. She is unshaped, undiscovered, unappreciated, in the way only a character from the Age of Riches can be.

I knew I'd found something special – not to the world, but to me. So here I am, at this moment, polishing her. She is, at least to me, a shining jewel.

This document – which I will annotate with my thoughts and perceptions – reads like a puzzle that begs to be solved but is determined to skip all the juicy clues. It makes little sense. It doesn't conform to any logic but its own. Things happen that could not possibly happen, and have meanings we could not possibly follow. The streaming side of me sees data: links and lines and numbers. Well, one number. But it can't make purpose from that. I think only my humanity can provide a reason for this dance. Romantic, I know. But aren't all quests on the romantic side?

I asked myself the same question over and over while reading: *What does this all mean?*

I'm beginning to think that's the wrong question to ask. What questions should I ask of it, and of that long-ago time that remains so well hidden under a wealth we cannot value? This is what lies at the heart of this personal project, and I hope, by the end, to have an answer.

The Dance of the Horned Road

the start—the rules—the lake—the mountain—the
breathing man—the others—the factory—the hotel—
the pub—the Spire—the doctor—the breathing
man—the cha—the cave of teeth—the forest—the twin
towns—the breathing man—the boat—the pavilion—
the forever—the farm—the swamp—the camper
van—the statue—the mud—the breathing man—the
tunnel—the walkway—the snack shack—the balloon—
the waiting room—the long room—the queue—the
robot—the decision—the rocket—the old friend—the
breathing man—the meeting—the escape pod—the
return—the heads—the switch—the escape—the start[3]

---

3 Are these chapter headings, or a possible corruption of
rudimentary digital metadata? There's no author name,
although the document is tagged as both *autobiography*
and *travelogue* so it seems acceptable to use Fairly as
the name of the creator, but with wariness – after all, other
tags applied to the document include fantasy, science
fiction, and adventure. Were they given at the time? Who
decides when a document earns certain tags?

FAIRLY FOUND HERSELF at the start of the horned road.

She had been daydreaming: daydreaming of not having to be the one who still waited—to be the one that time moved for. She couldn't remember the choice, the urge, to walk. To end up here.

She knelt and touched the surface. She had always assumed it was made of cobbles, small bulges of stone on their way to being worn smooth. But they were cold to the touch, and she wondered: were they made of some other material? Glass, perhaps? Or perhaps the cobbles, bunched and black, were warty growths on the back of a vast animal. A serpent. Or something with horns. How else would the road get its name? To walk on the back of a creature to whom she was no more than a tickle, a sliver of awareness: was that her fate?

This was it. The beginning of her adventure.

Fairly had first heard of the walking of the horned road at a party—a friend's birthday—when she was very young. The friend was called Cecile, and she had been newly eight, puffed up in a fresh pink dress. Cecile had been given a backpack, delicate, woven, with a picture of a rocket embroidered upon it, as a present from her parents, and when Fairly asked why, Cecile had replied: *For my quest.*

Wealth makes things move in the easiest direction, Fairly's mother had told her later that evening, after the party had ended. They had wealth, she realised, and her mother spoke from experience, somehow. Their house was large, and the feeling of financial comfort was a blanket over their casual movements, their languid goodnights. Her mother worked as a speaker. It was a lucrative position that came with respect, although Fairly hadn't realised that, and had thought there was some special light inside her mother that made others look at her with veiled, grateful eyes.

Later that month a storyteller had appeared at Fairly's own birthday party. He had worn a colourful, swirling cloak and had danced as he spoke, and she had swallowed every word like cake, her friends too, sitting in a ring around him. He had spoken of the road, and of adventures that awaited the brave, the chosen few.

381

How do I get chosen? Fairly had asked the storyteller, as he was packing away his cloak after the show. The other children had been playing a game, the tale already absorbed and accepted. The storyteller had shrugged, then said, *The time comes when the moment comes, and then you know. Or something.*

She had been thinking about it since, picturing some wonderful revelation, a world of sky-high starbursts and inner delight. Not a second like any other: one she couldn't pick out of the crowd. But when it came down to it, she had not been chosen at all. She had simply opted to make her way there.

Now, in the aftermath of choice, it was time to make her way back, and reveal what had happened.

She straightened and took a long look at the way the road began and ended at her village. It contained everything she knew, but from this perspective it was only an enclosed space between the thick wooden walls of a stockade[4], with a gate that opened in the morning and closed at night. Inside there were people so familiar to her that she did not even consider them to be separate from her own life: the mothers and fathers and children that had aged with her, and yet who never changed, never

---

4 Fairly lives in a walled village, which doesn't fit with what we think we know of the age. Why would her group, in particular, have isolated themselves this way? Not only to be alone inside their heads, but from the whole world? Could there have been many of these groups that simply appear to be invisible to the stream now, looking back at the age, because they were not represented digitally? *See: Information Poverty, Isolationism.*

talked to her in anything but the same tone of voice. Her mother was a speaker; their house was the heart of the village, of course.

The tasks, the buildings, the ground, the stream, the late-night gatherings for kind and social words, and the midday calls to the big hall for different words, words of business.

The study was quiet. It was a rare moment of peace, with the chime on the desk silent, as if the world knew to hold its breath.

'I've been chosen,' Fairly told her mother, who cried a little, and laughed, and took charge, with energy, of preparations.

No fake little bag with embroidery for Fairly: her mother drew out a sturdy canvas backpack with a small tent and a sleeping bag fitted, and a cooking pot and supplies attached to the base.[5] 'It was my own,' said her mother, and they hugged.

---

5 The backpack is hard to picture. How much weight can one human being carry? Maybe it's metaphorical. But I did find, through the stream, a document from the same period entitled *The Backpacker's Buddy: A Guide to Essential Packing for the Committed Rambler* (Author LG Vey, see: VEY96858889). Mainly it was formulated of anecdotes and nonsensical stories involving taking on bears and drinking one's own urine, but there was an extensive list of items that every backpacker should carry. This has been attached as Appendix A.

'A gift for a gift,' said her mother. 'That's the way to begin.'

381

THE DEPARTURE LOUNGE was empty.

Apart from Fairly. Alone, scared.

Her friends and family had only just waved her off and filed out. The mayor said: *Get cracking*, with a wide smile. *It's the best way. Hit the road early, move those feet.* So she had wished her mother goodbye, big hug, *You'll be back before you know it and you'll be all grown up, a hero*, and the others dispensed their own wisdom, then disbanded. She swallowed and swallowed. The fruit cake, specially cooked for the occasion by the village baker, had been very dry, and she hadn't wanted to wash it down with fizzy wine so early in the adventure. A clear head might well be needed for these first steps.

The departure lounge was in the village hall, which was the first and last building by the gate. It was a large, untidy room that she'd always taken for granted, having attended many of these leaving events. And returns, too, questers looking tired, grimy, spent. Older. Not everyone returned. She had asked her mother once, *What happens to the ones that don't return*? And her mother had said, *Not all roads lead back to the beginning.*

Quests were a funny business[6], all the more so for being given, as gifts, to those who were actually being asked— when she thought about it—to give up things.

Destiny was different. Destiny was an idea that Fairly decided she liked. She gave it to herself: a destiny. She wanted to find importance in being alive, and in walking the horned road. Let it lead where it would.

There were three things that now needed to happen. It was the way of the quest. Fairly did them with a sense of ceremony, even though there was nobody there to see it but herself. She took a mental picture of herself, to cherish later when things got tough.

She took the three cha that had been laid out on the table for her, next to the unappetising cake. She put them in the central pocket of her dungarees.

She picked up her inherited backpack and put it on. It was heavy; it contained objects that clunked, then settled

---

6 Quest narratives are well established throughout earlier ages and it is possible to make the assumption that a familiarity would be expected, although whether it would be on a fictional or non-fictional basis is not known. Did everyone have a quest? How did these get allocated? There's plenty of evidence showing a wealth of quest expectations made (often directly upon the young) in both real/fantastical terms, adding to the element of peril. What are the actual expectations here? Goals, attainment, wealth: these all appear in the document, and within life in the Age of Riches. In all ages, before this one, really.

into the shape of her back.

Then she thought about pressing the chain device.

381

THE MAYOR ALWAYS gave the same speech at leaving events. Fairly had thought repetition had rendered the words toothless, but for her own departure they had bitten hard:

> *Here, in this Land, we know Heroes by their*
> *actions.*
> *So we ask our young ones, the ones who dream,*
> *to complete a quest.*
> *The Quest is as follows:*
> *Press the button that sits atop every Chain Device*
> *in this land.*
> *You will be given three Cha. Use them wisely.*
> *You will be followed by the Breathing Man.*
> *You will find the way hard and long.*
> *And you will know your place when you are*
> *done.*

The device sat in the corner of the Conference Room. It was a large silvery box, and it was without adornment. A big red button sat in the centre of the top panel. The box looked very solid to her, as if she couldn't have picked it up, so she was glad that wasn't part of the challenge.[7] She wasn't strong, and she was only pretending to be brave; she already knew that. She didn't think this was necessarily a drawback to completing a quest, and perhaps it was a benefit. It gave her room to grow, and she had to start doing *that* by finding the courage to press the button.

Fairly had never seen anyone press the button. This part was done alone, always. It had occurred to her that maybe the box was capable of bestowing judgement, and carrying out an instant sentence—could it, possibly, zap those questers it decided could not possibly succeed? Disintegrate them, somehow, so there weren't even tiny pieces left? But no, surely the village wouldn't allow that to happen. She had faith in their protection of her, at least while she remained within the boundaries.[8]

Her legs felt as if they would barely hold her up, but

---

7 The poetic structure! I love it. I think it assumes, on the reader's part, a knowledge of traditional epics told in many languages. I've read a lot of epics. They're the best. The setting of goals ties strongly into earlier incarnations of quest narratives but is quickly undercut by the subsequent introduction of a machine both mechanical and allegorical – a literal 'device.' See documents on the fractious relationship between science and magic under SMG39485555.

8 The mechanical, then, gives way to the magical. Here we go.

she managed to walk up to the chain device and press the button, and at first it seems as though nothing has happened, but then I realise that the room has changed colour, just a little, shifting into brightness it did not possess before. I am braver. I see the world afresh, because I am a little taller, my eyes a little clearer.

This quest is off to a magnificent start.

381

THE FEELING MAKES it easy to walk the first mile.[9] The day is humid and my stomach is full with dry cake. I know what the chain devices look like, and I will find them all; oh yes, I will find them all.

I want to be more than I am.

I want to be everything to everyone. I want everyone to like me, and I don't see why that's impossible. I'll win the heart of every single person I come across on this quest.

The horned road is following the line of the hills. I

---

9 The function of the device is to change awareness, represented by a shift in person and/or tense. Did such devices have a real-life counterpart, and a literary switch represents some version of their function? Consciousness-altering objects could well have existed, although nothing like what we know today, and possibly without proper protection principles. A first hint of a perilous puzzle, this quest? Streaming without safety. But the stakes are so much higher – one life, one body. So romantic.

know this direction will lead me to the city, eventually. I've visited it once or twice, with my mother, when she was attending training courses for her job as a speaker.

I'll make the city, and all that lies beyond it, love me.

I think of Cecile.

She set out on her own quest over a year ago. She was always more mature than I, although only weeks separated our birthdates. She led the way, and I followed: in taste, in clothes, in sipping beer behind the village hall, in dancing without music, working out routines, trying to look like we didn't care if anyone watched. She hasn't yet returned. I dream for a while about meeting her on the horned road, and the two of us returning together, in victory, in knowledge.

Be every bit the hero you can be, my mother says on the chime, to those who call, in need of her help.

Only those on a quest are allowed to use the horned road. I won't meet anybody else, the kind of people who have made up my life so far, and that makes these first steps a lonely business, but I know if I continue in this direction, it won't be long until I reach the lake. I think about it as I take those first steps, beginning to feel the inescapable weight of the backpack: I will arrive and see it, and it will sparkle in the sunshine, and it will be long and cool and deep and perfect and this walk uphill is tiring and the cobbles of the road are slippery under the soles of my new boots and I crest the first big hill and see

381

I swim in the lake.[10]

The lake isn't cool. The water has been warming all day in the sun, and in the first few feet of its depths that heat has been retained, stored up, even though the day is now drawing to an end. I'll have to put up the tent soon, and roll out my sleeping bag, and find my first meal in my backpack. *This is my life,* I tell myself. *This is my life now.*

I take my languid time over my breaststroke.

The lake was the first place, the opening objective, and I'm here. An easy start, calm and peaceful. I swim further out into the silence, where the water darkens around me and the chill of the depths beneath begins

---

10 Another data corruption? The abrupt end of the previous section might suggest as much but the regularity in length of every section remains unbroken. Here's an interesting fact – every section of the document is precisely 381 words in length. That's the same number that appears in every gap in the narrative.

According to the Magnaman method, documents tagged with 381 are Business/Corporate/Economic (legacy). 381.381381381 is the tag for Philosophical and Ethical Principles of Defunct Economic Models. Not really relevant. Cross-referenced within the Age of Riches, 381 was a cyber expression with the meaning of 'I love you'. Three words, eight letters, one meaning. That's wonderful, isn't it? A number as an outpouring of love.

to permeate. The sun is sinking. The land and the road rise. That's my direction for tomorrow, but I'll stay here tonight.[11]

I have so very far to go.

The water is biting now, clamping on my legs, my chest. Icy. It is good and clean. It moves with me, under me; it holds me up. If only I didn't need air, or direction. I close my eyes and dive, certain of myself, and within seconds I am in a place so cold that I can't bear it. I have to surface. I force my frozen arms and legs into a crawl, and make it back to the lip of the lake. I will need to start a fire somehow. I think back over my lessons. It's all gone. I didn't even get a towel out of the backpack before I stripped off and waded in.

I'm beginning to understand that the world is not my friend. If the lake admits me, it can just as easily spit me out, or kill me. If twigs won't fall and a fire won't start, I will freeze.

---

11 Geographical cues have been followed within the text and streamed on the 600-million-plus representations of the world already found from that era to produce no conclusive evidence, but a possible topological match with an area found in then England with the lake in question being Bewl Water, a body of water found between the ancient counties of East Sussex and Kent. Bewl Water possibly existed as an actual location until the 2054 'Shaky Ground' incident, which may or may not have happened.

I find the matches[12], cast around for branches. I get lucky. I manage to light a match with my shaking hands, and the night is still warm enough that the branches catch without encouragement.

I'll never be so stupid again. I think of how very far there is to go, an unknowably great distance, and how different I will be by the time I reach the end of this road.

381

IN THE FIRELIGHT, wearing all my clothes, with the shivers finally abating, I pull out my three cha. I hold them in the palm of my hand, turning them over.

My cha are scarlet-painted pebbles, light on my palm.[13]

---

12 Matches are firestarters with romantic connotations of survival/desperation/danger. Start fires, fires burning, warmth, protection, danger.

13 The introduction of this hugely important concept to this document – cha – finds no immediate parallel in contemporaneous documents. Cha can refer to tea, a drink found in earlier ages that formed trade links across the colonised world. Repetition of the word (cha cha cha) creates a dance move dated to the islands/archipelagos of Cuba (nation-state – NST50978612) in the 1950s. Is the dance of the Horned Road the cha cha? Quest narratives often have strong links to embarrassment/torture that must be overcome, and public dancing could be both celebration and ritual humiliation. This is often found in Western visual creations of the age. Movies!

The colour is vivid; these are new cha. I put two back in my pocket and pick up the remaining one with thumb and forefinger to examine it in the firelight. It is a friendly delight, a depiction of a fabulous creature that reminds me of the fairy tales my mother used to tell me at night. It's been years, but I think I need one—a story of the little cha that protected us, our village, when we first put down our roots.

Cha have been a constant friendly presence in my life. I have a stuffed doll of one on the end of my bed. I wish I had brought it with me. I hugged it before leaving, told it to keep my room safe. That was a strange thing to say, maybe. I don't know who made my toy cha, but it was a red furry ball that I loved even in my earliest memories, just as I loved the tale of it. Some stories are protection in the darkest of nights.

I should have brought it along.[14] It hardly had any

Dance offs, dance competitions, learning to dance, a great big dance at the end. The body moves, expresses. One becomes two, pressed close, chest to chest. Two become a crowd.

14 How solitary existence must have been during childhood back then, with no connection to a streamed consciousness applied at birth, to grow with, learn with, become indivisible from. I am a we – so much of a we that we think of ourselves as I.

My favourite childhood toy was a soft rag with felt eyes. Not in a shape, not anthropomorphising, not human but

weight to it; it would not have burdened me much. I should have left something else out of the backpack. What, though? I need the food, the water, the cooking pot. I might have need of the emergency medical supplies and the change of clothes. The towel and the matches have already proven their use.

In the absence of the toy, I speak the story aloud, from memory. There are parts I don't remember, and parts that come to me complete, and they all get mixed in together to create a new whole that both comforts and unsettles me.

Afterwards, the night seems be listening to me, wondering if I'll dare say more. I feel watched. I feel vulnerable. I crawl into my tent, a triangle of scant protection, and make myself tiny in my sleeping bag, with my backpack beside me.

I am a hero, I remind myself, over and over again. *This is only the beginning.*

---

a movable, mutable rag that I could bend into any shape I liked, understanding so early on that it was about skin comfort, softness on the largest organ of the body. With the smell of lavender sunk inside, it was a delight. But it did not have the added responsibility of shielding me from loneliness, or imagination. I'm glad of that, but also certain that it means my experience of living is nothing like Fairly's experience, or any of the true humans who predate me.

MY FOLK HAD grandfolk, and they had grandfolk before them, and the grandfolk before that were the first people to come to this place and decide it should be a village. They had left the city behind, chasing a dream of a quieter life where hard work amounted to simple pleasure.

Little did they know, when they came to this spot, that it was already the home of a breathing man.

The breathing man slept in the rocks that they cracked open and the wood that they split apart to make their houses. They woke him with their destruction, thinking only to clear a space for themselves, not realising they were destroying the home of one who lived there already.

He shuddered awake, and seethed. He came to the villagers and breathed by each delicate ear in turn, and that cold breath changed them. They realised they were isolated, in a dangerous land they did not understand. They began to argue, and thought of returning to the city.

But a creature had followed them from the city. It was a cha. The cha were an ancient force in the world, long misunderstood. They could be mischievous and powerful, or they could be small and keen to help. This cha decided to help. It turned itself into three things: a pebble, a box, and a road.

The pebble bore its likeness, and to hold the pebble gave one the feeling of safety and connection.

The box was a solid silver cube that was topped with a button. To press the button gave one the feeling of perspective, realisation, singularity.

The road was a long path that the cha danced upon, and the breathing man saw the road and the dance, and found his feet at the threshold of the village before he could think twice. The Horned Road called to him. It gave him, as it gives to all it calls, the chance of adventure.

He set off after the capering cha, and neither ever came back.

The villagers rejoiced. Then they realised that some of their children, the very bravest and boldest, felt the pull of the dance too. They were sad, but they let the children go. They thanked the cha every day, and never forgot its good works.[15]

---

15 This section correlates with what I know of folk tales/ urban myths/warnings. Well-documented examples along similar lines can be found in, for instance, *The Pied Piper of Hamlin (Hamelin)* and *Cyber Weirdo (CHH38561006)*. These tales are truly chilling. Anything can be taken away in this age at a moment, even personal dignity. Sometimes I read the old documents under the horror tag, and wonder how they all thought up such horrible stuff. The age makes the individual, I suppose.

381

MORNING. ON I go. It would be good to meet someone. A travelling companion. Somebody to be on the road with. I find myself thinking about Cecile. I keep expecting to see her—not on her way back, her quest completed, but going my way, having waited for me. Nobody waits a year for another person, not even a person they love. And I didn't love her, so I can't imagine that she loved me, not really. We were sweet together, we made the grown-ups happy, but we both knew we weren't deep, forever friends.

The truth is, if she had waited for me, skulking about a few miles outside of the village for all this time, I would be delighted. Right now I'm thinking any company is better than no company.

I wonder if that would change if I got company.

I travel past the welcome shelter of that small wood, that friendly oak, and in the afternoon sun I'm surprised to find myself standing at a wooden signpost[16] that only

---

16 Signposts are everywhere in this document! And throughout the age, representing direction, hope, warning, and many other variations of pragmatic and symbolic meaning. I think it might be fair to comment that few thought about their direction through life/into the near future without some degree of trepidation. This area of study is well represented in the stream in *Read The Signs: A Semiotic Text* by Dr Xi, C.H. and *Not That Way, You Moron* by The Oceanic Collective. SIG59000430

points in one direction. It tells me there are five miles to get to Telezon[17].

Lots of the villagers take the front road to Telezon in order to trade, and from my own experience I know it's always a busy place. Many people arrive every day, converging to find new things, be new people, or just to work out new ways to get lost while sitting still, perhaps in a hotel room or a bar, perhaps at the races or at the public gardens at the base of the Spire, from which the rocket flies a few times a day.

I hear there are always jobs in Telezon, and I could get one, and spend some time making a little money to cushion the path of the horned road later. There's no rule that says I need to be endlessly journeying onward. Or perhaps 'There are always jobs' is one of those things they tell all heroes. *Experience life as it's offered to you, and it will offer you more*: that's one of the things my mother says on the chime, sometimes.

I won't stay long. I'll keep going on the horned road. *But it would be good to meet someone*, says my head. *Let's meet a city.*

---

17 No corresponding real-world name was found for this in the stream.

381

I SET UP my tent and complete the actions that are becoming familiar to me. Day four. Already I'm a professional at fending for myself. Somewhere off towards where the sun is setting, there is a picnic spot that I've camped at with my mother, on the hottest holiday I remember. The heat was so strong and later, when we got home again, a sheet of skin came off my shoulders.[18] It was as if the whole holiday ended at once, in a rush, refusing to sit on my back. I think I'll remember the satisfaction of that peeled skin all my life. *All my life.* I say it in my head like that's a long time, like this is the end of the adventure.

There is a ghost who lives near the picnic spot, which is a bench with a view over the lake I've left behind, but I have no other sense of direction regarding where or why it is, except that it's to the west. But is that to the west of the village? Who said that to me? It must have been my mother.

A ghost is the ultimate survivor.

Survivors know where to step, how to persist. Sleep here, walk there, keep my eyes down, and I could be a ghost. Perhaps it's wiser not to survive.

Human wisdom says: look, I can be complex and still make sense of myself, like the picnic spot; I can be

18 Search Illnesses of Climate Change (ICC224181488) for real horror. Oddly, not under the horror tag. Hm.

a destination that can't be found and the memory of a time when I was found. The sun can be so high, so strong: *I mark you*, it says, and then I sloughed it off and moved on. I want to be more than a survivor. I want to return home, and not get stuck there, repeating phrases like *all my life, all my life*.

I'm no ghost.[19]

In the morning I get up and walk on. I walk all day. I have my thoughts. I hold a cha in my palm. I feel so different, and my mind won't stop turning.

The road sweeps to the left, and there is the boundary wall.

---

19 Ghosts are brilliant. A classic human invention of life after death used for both solace and scariness. 'I'm no ghost,' within this context, takes on an extra level of meaning, for Fairly is a ghost of the age, one of so very many, insubstantial and only present in our consciousness if we allow her to be. It's so very moving to think she lives, for me, right now while I read. I can even think of her as an early version of the stream. I can access her! She's with me.

The bodiless spirit – would she have used 'ghost' as the term to describe the stream existences that reside now in the Unity Spire, or share human consciousness through upload into the corporeal form at birth, enabling a true cultivation and continuation of information from one organic generation to the next? *Artificial Intelligence* might have been the phrase used. Or it might have been cast in terms of demonic possession (DEV30067009). Fear of sharing the body, or control of the mind, predates the Age of Riches.

It marks the end of the land that my village demarcates as safe.

I made it.

I will sleep by the boundary wall tonight.

381

WEEDS.

Weeds grow strong in the shadow of the boundary wall. I end up pitching my tent among them. They are everywhere, sprouting from the cracks in the rough bricks, creating their own prickly carpet. I crawl into my tiny triangular space and squeeze into my sleeping bag, and I'm suddenly aware that they are underneath me, resisting me, refusing to be squashed down. The roots of them are not cowed, either; they know they'll win this fight. They are waiting for their moment to spring back, just as soon as I roll up my possessions and move along. There is malevolence in their hardiness, their disinterest. Can I hear them growing?

Only in the long, boring stretches of the night could this happen.

The sound of growing.

But I sleep, eventually, because that's what we all do. Eventually.

And then I wake.

To the sound of

Breathing

Breathing
Not my breathing
On the other side of the thin wall
Inches from me
An inch from me
Breathing
Breathing
The breathing man
He's here to get me
The breathing man
He's here to kill me
I cannot move
I cannot breathe
But he can breathe
The breathing man.

It's dark as I've ever known it, it's the darkest night I've ever felt, it's never going to get to dawn. I won't make it through this dark, this sound, this man. This night. This night. This night

And slow
And slow
And slowly
It gets lighter
It gets lighter
It gets light

Birdsong is louder than the breathing, his breathing, my breathing

I find a way to move my stiff and frozen bones

I get up, and unzip, and make breakfast, and pack things away, and uncover the weeds beneath the tent. They spring back into perfect shape, as if I was never there, and a moment later I start walking and they are right: I was never there at all.

Where is he?

They said the breathing man would follow me, but I thought it was a—I don't know, a story, a myth. Like the cha.

I keep looking over my shoulder.

Will he always, now, be here?

If I am going to be a hero, is he going to be my villain?

This journey comes with a breathing man.[20]

---

20 The villain arrives. I can easily hate the breathing man. He bears some resemblance to the ghost concept as introduced earlier. His presence affects the shape of the story, drawing it out, pressurising it into short, tight sentences. Fairly decides he is necessary, perhaps because of the rules that were established at the commencement of the quest.

Who is the breathing man? What does he represent? Did every quester really get their own allocated man to follow them about? How would that work within the nation-state separatist framework? This raises fascinating questions (that I can't answer!) regarding economic impact and employment levels. If he is a literary/metaphysical construction, then we have the choice to view him as symbolic or spiritual, or to cast him in the role of 'other.'

I LEAVE THE boundary wall behind and the horned road begins to climb. It gets steeper and steeper, rockier underfoot, and eventually I realise I'm walking up a large hill—dare I even call it a mountain? when does it become a mountain, or is that a decision for the person walking it?—and the air is getting thinner and colder, and the backpack straps are cutting into my shoulders. I take out my warm coat and carry on, climbing, for hours, and every time I stop I look behind me and see... nothing that shouldn't be there.

Is he there?

I expect a view upon reaching the top of this mountain; I want to see a vista that will give a multicoloured map of the way behind and to come. But no, the clouds coagulate as I climb higher, and when I reach a plateau there's only mist: fine, drenching, collapsing visibility to barely beyond the end of my toes. I feel like I'm floating. I inch forward and follow the road as it begins its descent. Eventually the rocks smooth out to a solid path once more, and the mist clears to reveal yet another sunny afternoon, and a dip into a wooded valley with a stream crossing the way. I take off my boots and let

(For further discussion of the pervasive role of othering/ otherness as a classical 'divide and conquer' mechanism in The Age of Riches see YNM59381039.)

the icy water wash away the hard walking. Then I find fruit on the trees, and I eat four of them, finding one has been wasped. It contains great holes in its succulent flesh, right through the skin, and I didn't notice.

I sit down under a tree and close my eyes for a moment, just a moment.

I don't remember my mother ever telling me much about the breathing man.

I can't recall her speaking about it on the chime, but she must have, surely, in those calls when the quester was desperate, panicked; she had a special voice for such people, quiet and firm and full of sympathy. Could it be her advice, on those occasions, related to this circumstance? What was it she used to say?

When I wake, I feel him close again, as if this day was hide and seek, a game we played, and I jump up with my heart pounding in my chest, and run.

381

ALL RUNNERS MUST stop, or burst.

I stop, catch my breath, doubled over. I don't dare to look behind me. By chance I see a cluster of tents nearby behind an outcrop of rock: blue, orange, red.

'Hello?'

Three of them, sitting in the triangle of grass between the tents. They are different in skin colour, in clothing, but about my age, I think. It makes it harder to approach them; if they were older, I would go to them and say: *help me*. But this means I still must help myself.

'We know,' they call. 'We know. He's out there.'

They tell me they've all seen him, been followed by him since leaving their own villages.

'All of you?' I manage to say. They pass me a cereal bar, an apple.

'He doesn't come if we're together,' they say. 'He hasn't shown up since we've been together.'

'How long is that?'

'Three days.'

Three days, and they've formed a unit. I get the feeling they'd let me stay tonight, walk with them tomorrow. Something about it feels like an easy choice. But aren't we meant to all go alone? I don't say it, but I think it, as they tell me about the sound of the breathing man, and their plans to do everything as a group to keep him away.

'Stay,' they say. 'Be safe.'

And I do. I stay for that afternoon, that night. I pitch the tent close to their triangle, and we swap information. Their lives are remarkably like my own, and although I am scared—and I am very scared—I feel better knowing the breathing man has come to us all.

It's part of the journey.

'We'll be safer in numbers,' they say, and I realise that's not true—what difference does it make? If he wanted to hurt us, he could do it easily no matter how many there were. We are so weak, so young. Look at us, crying, huddling.

I have a good night's sleep, and the next morning I wake early, listen to my slow, steady breathing, and steel myself. I pack up my tent before they surface, and I'm on my way. I'm amazed at myself, my own strength, and I wonder how long it will continue to grow.[21]

381

SOMETIMES I THINK I've given him the slip.

Not today, though. Today I know he is only just behind the last bend, because I've not managed to make good time over this rocky ground, but finally the road is flattening out once more and there is a building up ahead. It's a large grey box with tall chimneys—a factory, maybe? I've seen them on the outskirts of Telezon before. Smooth smoke is streaming up to the cloudy sky, and a light rain is falling.

I head for it. Actually, the truth is, I seem to end

---

21 Personal growth of the hero as opposed to those who are not up to the task! I think this is a classic quest ideal. Fairly is brave (braver than I could ever be) whether the foe is real or imagined. (It is possible to argue that imaginary foes are much harder to defeat but easier to picture overcoming; does this explain the proliferation of unreal adversaries at a time when so many problems existed in reality?)

up aiming for it, and as I pass the gates the instinct overwhelms me and I decide I should go in. They are open, just enough to admit me, but there are no guards, no sign of anybody else. The long rows of windows are blackened. All the glass is opaque—how does air get in? I push open the double doors and find myself in an area where corridors converge. A desk sits at the crossroads. Behind it, the longest corridor leads to a vast, open hall filled with silent machines. Nobody in sight. On the desk there's a chime, like the chime in my mother's study[22]—a

---

22 Is this a quaint throwback? Many documents state that the 'telephone' was invented in 1876 by Alexander Graham Bell, and Fairly's chime bears similarities, although all calls seem to go only to her mother. I was delighted to find the first telephone call commenced with the phrase 'ahoy' which relates to sea travel – a concept that becomes relevant later in the narrative. The ideas wrap around each other, feed into each other: I feel like we're gathering speed. On land, on water, floating on air; so many ways to travel in a body, over bodies.

Also: the difficulties of communicating between generations! Streaming solves this, but to work without corrupting the free associations of the organic brain the streamer lies in a dormant state of non-influence unless accessed. It provides information, but it does not extrapolate. Are we, truly, then, in communication with all that has gone before, or is this a one-way process? I find this to be a really interesting reflection between ages.

Reflections on the face of the water. Ahoy.

receiver squatting on a cradle, deflated. It bears a layer of dust.

I've never been allowed to touch a chime before.

I pick up the receiver, disturb the dust. I wet my lips, bring the circle of dots in the centre of the receiver to my face, and I say, 'Hello.'

HELLO

says my own voice, so loud, echoing, reverberating through the reception, through the hall. I slam down the receiver. It's like being stung, this level of reaction. Looking around for the thing that has pierced me. I'm looking for him. But it was my voice, some sort of communication system.

What if everything is this empty?

What if Telezon is abandoned? If the world has ended while I've been walking?

I leave. I walk out of the building, out of the gates. I should have stayed with the others. I am so lonely, and yet everything within me screams that I'm being watched. This is hard. This is the hardest thing I've ever done, and it is still the beginning. Still the beginning.

381

FROM THAT ONE factory—which seems, now, to have been waiting for me—the human world grows. It expands into more buildings that erupt from the stretched ground, and which show signs of movement, of life. Slowly the beginnings of Telezon coalesce, and as the road leads me through the outskirts, to sights I begin to find familiar, I start to feel like I'm getting somewhere.

It's sudden, the change from rural to industrial to central, and there are no more fields, no more factories. Other people cross the horned road, use it as if it is any usual road, and at first I look at them, their clothes and colours[23], but they are not interested in me and I learn to keep my head down, to maintain an urban level of detachment. All the time an excitement is waking inside me. *I love this city,* I remember. Trips when I was so little, and there was ice cream in a shop. *I love this place.*

As the evening begins to descend, it occurs to me that I don't have to put up my tent, eat my rations. In fact, it would look strange if I did. I'll find a hotel. I look for one, and there it is:

---

23 Is this a suggestion of a multicultural hub? The city could be seen as a central point of experience – all human life was there. People arrived, swelled its numbers, fed into its streets and buildings. The crowded city as a destination that draws in both the great and the gullible exists as a narrative predating the Age of Riches. Watch *Stupid State of Mind With The Big Three Million – An Exercise in Artificial Group Think* to gain an approximated experience of city life (CIT23994374).

HOTEL HORN
For Weary Ones

It has a neon sign and it looks cheap but happy, the pink curtains in the windows like smiles, pulled up at the corners, and it's good enough for me.

I check in, ask about a room.

'One cha,' says the woman. She is not as cheap and happy as the hotel. She has a weary, grasping look. She tells me she can give me a room with a view over the Spire[24], and throw in dinner and breakfast, and I go for it, even though I only have three cha and to lose one this early is... yes, it's a con. Not a good deal. I'm certain of it, but I need to rest, at least for one night. A door with a lock, safe from the breathing man.

I sleep deeply, and eat a bacon roll, and I move on to find the city was up before me and is into its business.

---

24 Spires have a religious connotation from earlier eras that stretch into the Age of Riches, often corrupted to represent a really tall, pointed building. That usage persists to this day; for instance, the Unity Spire project of the Age of Curation. Some ideas link us throughout time! It's hard for me to picture the Spire in this document as anything but a portentous place, filled with meaning for Fairly, for that is how the Unity Spire (that symbol of global human/streamer accomplishment) seems to me in my time. I feel bound to her by this concept, because it represents the beginning and end of one kind of journey.

I wander for hours. I will return to the horned road later.

381

THIS IS SUCH an obvious place. Designed to take advantage of me and my kind, the heroes in making, the questers. Preying on our weakness.

The Hotel Horn. What a con.[25]

I shouldn't have done it. My pocket feels so much lighter. Only two cha left.

And who's to say they weren't in league with the breathing man? He could have taken the room next door, laid with his head inches from mine, separated only by a thin wall and two headboards, and he would be there, ready for me to open the door, head down for my breakfast, cheap bacon, bad rolls. I could have seen him sitting opposite me, felt that cold sting of recognition. Would I recognise him? I feel certain I'd know him.

I am an idiot. Just one of many in this city, no doubt, which once felt benevolent—has it changed? I head to

---

25 Heroes must also make foolish mistakes – the perfect hero would hold little interest for those who live in an imperfect world, such as Fairly. Perhaps this is why quest narratives are no longer popular in our age; we would have to find a way to empathise with discord when we have sacrificed so much to eradicate it.

the financial district and walk between the tall square buildings. A hot air balloon glides overhead—what a sight, yellow and red! I eat my lunch in a small park at a place near the docks, with boats big and small to watch, sailors at work.

After a long day of blaming myself, I find myself walking in the direction of the Spire.

The crowd begins to thicken up, take on form, and I push into it. I hit the tourist streets with their outside tables and promises of live music later. There's a bar that catches my eye for its honest name:

Old Joe's

It has a worn but a clean frontage, with concertina doors that have been pushed back for tables half in, half out. I sit on a stool, not far from the door, and eye the barman. He looks familiar.

'What can I get you?' he says, and I could order a beer, or a wine. Something strong. I think he'd buy it. I'm an adult now. When it comes time to pay up, I could make a run for it. I'm about to become a criminal, all for the sake of a blurry moment. And I don't even like the taste of alcohol—at least, not the fizzy wine they serve at home. I picture my mother and the mayor clinking glasses at my leaving party.

'I'VE GOT NO money,' I say, 'but I'm on a quest.' I've no idea how this works. Nobody has discussed how to actually survive. I'm only just realising that.

'Yeah,' he says, still not looking at me. 'The backpack kinda gives you away.' He pours a white wine and puts it in front of me. 'It's on the house.'

I sip the wine. It's acidic and unpleasant. I should have eaten first. Aware of his eyes on me, I fetch a cereal bar from my backpack and unwrap it.

Someone else comes to the bar and asks for beer. The barman serves, settling into a regular rhythm of custom and customers. Demand picks up as I nibble and sip, but I feel his eyes return to me often.

'How are you finding the road?' he says.

'It's okay.'

'Oh. Yeah. Of course. I'm Sam.'

'Fairly.'

'It gets busy,' he says. 'You need a room? You can have the upstairs room if you'll do some serving in the evenings. I'll throw in a meal.'

'I'm passing through,' I say, and he shrugs. Then I say, 'Is it okay if it's just for a couple of days?' and he says, 'Yeah. That's how it usually works.'

So I agree, and now I know how it usually works, which is an added bonus. Work for a few days, then move on. I'm part of a process that I feel I'm beginning to understand.[26]

'Come on, then,' Sam says, and I hop off the stool and move to the business end of the bar. It's a steep learning curve. I like it. I like pouring drinks and watching people get a little happier, and a little happier again, until the point they're too happy and they collapse into puddles of sadness.

At the end of the night my clothes smell of beer and sweat, and I feel like I've become part of something. I can't sleep in this small, airless room. I open the window as wide as it will go and listen to the last of the revellers stagger away, and I'm still there when the sun comes up.

Is this why some of us don't return home? We find a place that suits us, and we stay there?

Does this place suit me?

––––––––––

26 The beginning of grasping the rules of the game as Fairly's life expands into the concept of the city. She continues to change, but what about her remains the same?

I was twelve years in body, on a walking holiday along the coast with my mother, both of us using our legs, feeling them tire. It was a good feeling. She was asking me about my socialisation classes, and how they were progressing. We stopped and ate apples. I looked far out to sea, past the energy farms, to that clear blue space, and I thought: *I can be anything. I can become anything.*

381

I WORK IN the bar, and I watch the people drink, and time passes.

In Telezon, time does not move unless the people say so, and they are all in agreement that it should move, and move fast. They run; they are speedy, on the treadmill of time they create, and I admire them for their urgency, and their ability to live according to this collective decision.

In Telezon, interest is money, and money makes interest. I talk to the customers, and I listen to their animated conversations, in which everything is important right now. I learn that everybody has a hobby that creates experience. Certain clothes must be worn, certain items must be purchased, manipulated, upkept. I get into the habit of drinking coffee, mid-morning, in the park, and I see them cycling past on expensive bikes, in skin-tight clothes. Everything must be just right, accessorised for this activity.[27] Even the drinks and snacks agree, in Telezon.

I am bemused, and I wait for the future to arrive on its own terms. Will I stay another day, or will I start walking? I don't know yet.

---

27 If cha is tea, then what is coffee? See: java, dirt, joe, mud. Muddy puddles? Muddy intentions? And what is cycling? Upcycling, downcycling, cyclic weather. Cycles of thought. Round and round in muddy circles.

I could take up cycling. It would give me friends, an identity. Or maybe the act of watching others cycle is enough. Can watching people make a person interesting? But it begins to dawn on me that nothing is really happening to me while I am watching other people. I don't even think very much about the breathing man anymore. I haven't seen him. Or maybe I have, but I don't know him. Maybe he looks a little like everyone else, here in this city. I could serve him in the bar, and he would not stand out from the others.

I do not fit in.

Do I want to?

I've started to like my little room, with the window thrown open and the sounds floating up. I can picture all the questers that have come before me. I can imagine the ones that will come after.

I'm starting to forget how much I hate the tent, and the food of the road. I picture myself walking away, moving on, with a backpack filled up with new supplies. This is not the place where I stop.

But I don't go yet. Not quite yet.

381

AFTER MY COFFEE in the park, I usually take a stroll to the Spire.

It is a tourist centre and a business hub. The Spire also

attracts pilgrims, who are at pains to have nothing to do with the tourists or businesspeople. They are easily spotted by headbands they wear, which bear two little triangles, set apart, pointing upwards to the sky. They are in awe of the Spire. I know next to nothing about their beliefs, but I know I'm in awe too. So tall, so thin. It stretches up into the sky. I can't even see the top, most days, obscured in cloud, but on the best days I can see the rockets spurt from the tip and set off to far planets. A rocket leaves three times a day, and I watch the lunchtime-scheduled one. It is red and white, and it shines in the sun.[28]

---

28 Space flight! Yes, the hub of the science fiction adventure and the cornerstone of twenty-second century disparity politics. 'Those who can, do it in space' was a global advertisement campaign slogan in 2175 (as the rush to escape the ramifications intensified for those still invested in decaying financial systems) but the data I've accessed so far suggests that routine commercial space flight was not really viable at this time – a realisation that dawned globally after the Moon Base Meltdown of 2186, in which a number of 'superheroes' died while trying to save the president's granddaughter. I like to view it as a dream of escape tying back to earlier ideals of open spaces/vast plains of adventure. (See: Westerns, seafaring, expansion goals under LLP39560395)

The contentious era of space flight lost its grip on fiction/ non-fiction by the end of the twenty-second century to be replaced briefly by the idea of instant matter relocation.

Imagine the journey, imagine leaving the Earth. What lives the rich live. I could never get tired of watching such affluent grace.

The pilgrims feel the same.

Today, two of them share my usual bench. They unpack sandwiches. The triangles on their thin headbands stick up. They remind me of the tiny, perky ears of the cha.

No physical evidence of achieving this (or being altered at an atomic level to become a 'superhero') remains; over 300,000 dedicated groups of curators work in this area alone in the hope of finding evidence. Perhaps the stream is a superhero, searching for its ancestors? I like that idea. Super evolution.

Why did space flight lose its gleam? The build-up of space junk, the realisation of the impossibility of conquering the distance involved, the sheer expense involved, fear of alien invasion: all these factors have been blamed. But imagine. Imagine taking to the sky, and beyond, to the unknowable. Freedom. The word means so many things to so many people. I'm not sure why it comes to my mind now.

Freedom.

When I thought: *I could be anything*… did that include becoming a hero, super or otherwise?

See Chan, P.F., *Caped Chronology* (CAC06978900) for further insights into how aspects of 'superhero' culture infiltrated, then dominated, mainstream discourse, creating the unsolvable problem of the verisimilitude of its own origin story.

The one closest to me offers me a sandwich after the rocket has left, and says, 'We're learning more from this than from a year of theology classes.' There's a lot here I don't understand. How is watching learning, and what is there to be learned? But then I remember most of my education involved watching someone in the act of talking to me about things they also hadn't done. Mister Ellenby taught all the kids, mainly about village life. Was I ever engaged with the things he told me?

And if I'm not learning anything now, why I am watching the Spire?

I ask the pilgrims where they came from, and they name a place I've never heard of. 'Over the sea,' one says helpfully. 'We heard there are spare tickets, sometimes. Cheap. Even free, for the right sort of people. Have you heard that?'

'No.'

'Imagine,' he says. 'Imagine flying up there and taking the good word with you.'

I wonder what the good word, the best word, is. But I don't ask.

381

IT'S ONLY THE next day when I meet a man who offers me a ticket for free.

He sits next to me on the bench, and he looks just like a

businessman, in a good suit, with a briefcase. He crosses his legs and I notice his black socks. So black. As if new to the world that day.

'Lovely day,' he says. 'I've seen you here before, haven't I? You want to go up there?'

I don't answer.

'I work for a company,' he says. 'They send me out here to look for good candidates. For relocation. So many planets need bright young minds. What do you think? Think you're up to the challenge?'

I don't believe in his opportunity, or in his smile, which speaks to me of other things. *Imagine going off with this guy, imagine being that stupid,* some wise old part of my mind that I can't remember ever hearing in my head before says. I am getting more cynical. I sound like a patron of the bar, at the end of a long day in which everyone was out for themselves.

I turn him down—with an apology, because I'm weak and young and afraid to offend, no matter what my mind says to me now on the sly—and I walk away quickly.

Later, in the bar, I tell Sam about it. He says, 'Yeah, some kids accept. I've heard about it. Nobody ever sees them again, you know?'

'Maybe they went to a different planet,' I say, wanting to believe it. He raises his eyebrows at me.

That man has made me so angry. He turned my life into a test that other people were allowed to judge. Only stupid kids go with him, right? Only desperate kids. How can it be that he is allowed to walk around under the Spire and talk to those who are trying to dream in peace? *If there was anything criminal going on, someone would do something*, the old part of my brain says. The village part.

The new part says: *yeah, right*.

I serve myself a white wine and sip it between serving all the Telezon people who are better at living than I am. I'm getting a taste for that wine. Dry. Tart.

381

I AM AWARE I'm waiting. Changing. Waiting for the change to be complete.

Something will come along.

Eventually, an illness comes along. Only a sneeze. But Sam tells me I can't work while I'm sneezing away in people's faces, and he gives me evenings off, spent lonely in my upstairs room, and when the sneeze doesn't clear he gives me the address of a doctor. 'Probably free for your sort,' he says. I'm not sure if he means questers or kids or bar staff. I'm not sure what my sort is, any more.

The doctor says, 'It's an allergy.'

I ask him what I'm allergic to, and he says he could do tests, rule out things. 'I see it a lot in young people like you,' he says. 'Arriving in Telezon. Not used to the

61

atmosphere here. The toxins. You might acclimatize. You might not.'

So now I know. I'm a young person and I'm currently allergic to Telezon.

'Nice fresh air is best for you,' he says. 'That's what you're used to.' But he writes me a prescription for a nasal spray to try, and tells me to wait in reception while he gets the practice manager to sign it off as care for the vulnerable. I don't really understand what that means either. What any of it means. Where am I going? I'm sitting in reception, that's right, I'm sitting there waiting to be given something. A spray to make things better, somehow.

Mainly I feel like sneezing a lot.

It's a very long wait.

I try to smile at the other people who come and go. They are older, often, and they carry themselves as if they have heavy things inside. I picture stones and grief and excess water. I'm glad to be me—yes, that's the feeling. Glad to be young and allergic. I'm just deciding not to wait any longer for the nasal spray when a man enters the reception and takes a seat opposite me, and he catches my eye and returns my smile so readily that I feel I must know him.

He leans forward, and he breathes out.

The breathing man.

Is he the breathing man?

I can't tell. I don't know this either. But I think it might be the breathing man.

381

MY SMILE WON'T leave. It's glued to me. I don't want to smile at him, but I can't make it drop. I'm stuck in this pose. I can't speak. I'm rigid in the chair, dry and brittle and so hot, so cold.

He looks away. He has a moustache, a fat dark shape balancing on his lip, and he's wearing glasses with thick lenses. Is this a disguise? He breathes out loudly once more, shifts in his seat, then coughs. He has a cough. And a cold. I can hear it in the rattle of his throat.

I don't think he is the breathing man.

The practice manager calls my name, and hands over a sealed paper bag. He looks at me with disapproval, but he seems too busy to sustain it for long, and everyone has already lost interest in me by the time I reach the door. The man who might have been the breathing man isn't even looking my way anymore.

I walk.

Telezon is so big and busy that, for a while, I lose myself in it, and within my thoughts. Why can I not remember precisely what the breathing man looks like? If I can't bring his face accurately to mind, then he could be anyone, be anywhere. I'm so stupid. I should have kept him in the forefront of my thoughts at all times. I never should have got lulled into Telezon life.

I remember the mayor's words. How could I have pushed them to the back of my mind?

> *You will be followed by the Breathing Man.*
> *You will find the way hard and long.*
> *And you will know your place when you are*
> *done.*

He's meant to follow me.

It is his job.

The horned road connects us. It's a string that links us together. The string will always pull tight.

I don't recognise this part of the city. It's small, and unfriendly. It doesn't want to admit me. I turn around and around, expecting to find his face before mine at any moment, and see the Spire rising up from the buildings. I head for it, and Telezon begins to unravel into the familiar. That shop, surely? That corner, and the chairs and tables. I must be near the horned road again.

381

WALKING WITH THE pretence of purpose, I come across another chime.

It's in a yellow booth, glass-paned, just big enough to admit one person. People walk past it and around it as if it's natural, like a tree. But it's incredible to me; a direct link to my mother's desk, in her study, at home. It's as if she just walked past me in the street. I can smell her.

I am not only connected to the breathing man. I'm also connected to my village, and my mother. I can speak to her.

I walk to the booth and stand within its yellow walls.

A notice above the chime, printed in precise ink, reads:

FOR EMERGENCY QUESTER USE ONLY

I pick up the receiver, and say, 'Hello? Hello?' feeling like an idiot, which is becoming a pretty standard feeling for me.[29]

'Hello?' says a voice, my mother, my mother, and I keep saying hello at her until she says, 'What's the matter? Can you tell me?'

---

29 Is Fairly an idiot? She is lost/we are lost. If she is, we all are. The breathing man follows her. Perhaps he follows us all. I was in a sculpture garden, touching materials shaped into meaning, a few days after first reading this document. I put my hands on a rough, round stone with a hole through its centre. It was hard, black. I felt I could finally put a name to the feeling that has dogged me. Something is wrong: this feeling transcends time, links us all. Something is wrong with me (us) and I don't know how to explain it, let alone put it right. Is this how the reader is meant to feel? Does this emotion span the ages?

I would say many things, but I can't manage to get any of the words out. My throat has closed over with emotion, and I can't cry, I can't burst. This is a public street. What will people think? So, into the silence, she puts her own words, soothing and familiar. I've listened to her field these kind of chime calls a thousand times. She says:

The way looks the worst just as it's about to level out.

She says:

You have nothing and everything to prove, and only you can work out what that is.

She says:

Chin up, best foot forward, chest out, clear eyes, strong stomach.

Or something like that—I'm not really listening at this point, not to the words. Just to her voice. She has me safe in the sounds she makes. Who cares what she says?

Then she says:

Dear, I have to go, I have another call. Go. Go live your life. Go live your life.

The chime falls into silence.

I replace the receiver, step back from the booth, and see the city with fresh eyes. Yes, I know where I am. The bar is just around this corner, and my sneeze has gone. I can work tonight, and I'll pack up and go in the morning.

381

SAM SAYS, 'I'M surprised you stayed so long,' and nods goodbye. How easily he welcomes and farewells. I suppose another quester is coming down the road toward him right now.

I swing by the Spire on my last morning, and on a whim, approach the ticket stand by the archway. A woman in a blue outfit and matching hat smiles at me and asks if she can help. I enquire about the price of a ticket, and she frowns and says, 'But they're not for sale,' as if I should know this. There are so many things I should know. Who is at fault here? My elders, my village, myself? I remember my mother's soft voice and try not to blame her a little bit for my complete lack of preparation.

I had a vision of being looked over, told to pass, gifted with a ticket to take me far away from here to a place where the breathing man can't follow. But I can see quite clearly that things simply don't occur along those lines. Outside, the two pilgrims I met before are looking at me with wet, anxious eyes. 'You're not taking him up on his offer, are you?' one of them says, and I reassure them, and tell them I'm leaving.

They point in the direction of the coastline.

'We own a stretch,' they say. 'Our private order. It's so peaceful. Retreat there, for a little while. Get away from this terrible city of sin.'

'Are you leaving?' I ask them, and they say, 'Oh, no.'

Then they say, 'You can stay at the order for free, if you work.'

I'm beginning to understand that work is only free to those who aren't doing it, but I let it slide, and I thank them, and I think about the coast as I make my way back to the road.

It turns out the horned road heads in the direction of the coastline anyway. Good. I have a desire to see the sea. I've seen a lake and a river, but never an open stretch of sea, and the thought of it is enough to lift my spirit and get me through that first day as a quester on the move again, tent in backpack, food in sealed bags.

381

IT'S A BUSY path out of Telezon, and at first I keep myself to myself. People have ways and wiles, and any of them could be in disguise.[30] Once I've had that thought, I can't keep it out of my mind. I start to think about making my own disguise. A big, fierce one. This journey would surely be easier that way.

No trades, no conversations.

---

30 Even if she is an idiot, she has learned to look upon others with scepticism. Change is happening. I can't always see it, but I must believe it. I'm changing. The document is changing me.

Then, suddenly, I'm in clear air and the smell of Telezon seems far behind me. Up ahead there are mountains, and I wonder if I've turned, or if I was never really heading for the coast at all.

A family walking ahead of me—too fast to be overtaken, too slow to be avoided—includes a small boy, who notes my gaze on the mountains. 'The big mountain has teeth,' he tells me. 'It's famous. It eats people.'

'Mountains don't eat people,' I tell him, and he gives me that look—the look I get a lot. I must be unsound, somehow.

'It ate my grandmother,' he says. 'The things up the mountain did. That's what my dad said.'

Do dangerous things live in mountains? Does it make a difference if I am eaten by the very big or the very small?

The boy runs back to his family, and I see him pulling at his father's sleeve, telling him all about the silly girl who doesn't believe in being eaten. I wonder if it will lead to another conversation, a grown-up one in which I am told more things I ought to already know, but the father shrugs off the son and they walk on in front of me.

Where the horned road forks, they head down towards the coast.

That can't be right. There aren't meant to be turnings on the horned road. Which way am I meant to go? I panic until I get a little closer, and then I see it: two curving shapes beside the road that leads up to the mountain. The curves are built of pebbles, carefully placed, in the wiry grass. They must be meant to represent horns, surely. How fragile this signpost is. Some of the pebbles have been kicked out of place. I take the time to replace them. By such actions are roads defined.

381

I TAKE THE high road and settle into my stride, leaning forward, counterbalancing the weight of my backpack. I am a walker once again. A quester. I'm thankful for my good boots.

I wouldn't mind being swallowed.

I think about it as I take my steps: one, two, one, two. Not to be consumed. Only to be taken in, incorporated. Part of a bigger, better thing. The city wasn't right for me, but—a mountain?

I wonder if I'm allergic[31] to all swallowing experiences,

---

31 Yuck. Allergies. Problems of the body. It would not have been at all unlikely for Fairly to exhibit several symptoms including excessive sneezing, coughing, a tight throat or chest, itchy eyes, or rashes. Imagine attempting to live with all that on a daily basis. It's possible that physical discomfort was so prevalent for urban populations that they simply ceased to catalogue it, in the main. Or possibly it did not fit with personal ideals of

or if a mountain would be exempt.

I walk onwards, getting higher. It's only a short time since I climbed that first mountain and found no view at the top. I thought then I could say: *I have climbed a mountain.* But actually, looking at the size of this place, that was really only a hill, at best. Up there, everything was shrouded in mist. I wonder what will be at the top of this bigger, better challenge. Or perhaps all mountains look bigger in the future, and become mere hills in the past.

I see a creature.

It's a small red lump. I could have mistaken it for a stone, but then it moves, and dashes away at speed. It has fur, long back legs that give it a lolloping movement, and two triangular ears high on its head. It's cute. It reminds me of a cha.

---

heroism. This might also explain why many documents already investigated do not mention online/instantaneous communication, choosing to ignore it although it was global at this point. That which is ubiquitous hardly seems worth a mention, and isn't a heroic issue. Fairly is given the additional challenge of only being able to access communication on specific occasions through the chime; would a quest with all the help one can get be a useless endeavour?

How, then, could one realistically become a quester then – or now? If I want to undertake my own quest, what could that look like? I feel robbed of opportunity.

It surely can't be dangerous.

As I continue to climb I see them more and more, and they get used to me. They don't run away so fast, taking their time to nibble the grass, apparently enjoying the sunshine.

But the sunshine passes, and the evening draws in, and I learn that the weather in the mountains is unpredictable. It's going to get cold, I can tell. That's fine—I have my sleeping bag—but I'm not relishing the idea after the little bedroom above the bar. How warm it was, how safe.

The creatures are massing.

They stand in a group, lined up, ahead of me. Blocking the road. I stop walking and stare at them.

The one in the middle, the biggest one, gestures at me. It stands on its back legs and beckons with a furry front paw.

Then they all hop away, as one.

381

FOLLOW US, IT meant. I'm sure of it.

So I follow them. They never go so fast as to leave me behind. Occasionally they stop hopping and turn their adorable heads and check I'm still with them.

Lead me, I think.

They lead me to a chalet.

It's set back slightly from the road, but I wouldn't have found it without their help. It's a beautiful wooden construction, with long sheets of glass looking out over the pastures that slope back to the sea. A creature hops up and down next to a small collection of pots by the door, and I lift them one by one until I find a key. I let myself in and stand in bright luxury for a moment. This is elegant. Tastefully decorated, light woods and open beams.

Investigation reveals four bedrooms with patchwork quilts on the big soft beds, a brushed steel kitchen, running water in a blue bathroom, and a heated swimming pool. Out the back there's a hot tub, too.

Make yourself at home, I think the creatures are saying with their body language. So I do. They sleep beside my bed that night, after having made me a nutritious salad. And when I wake the following morning and find it has not been a dream, I dig out my cha, the symbols of protection, and examine them next to my benefactors. Yes, they are the same. Cha do exist. Here they are, small and red and fluffy and caring for me, a quester.[32]

---

32 Cha transmute from dead material to living creatures. Back and forth from fantasy to reality they hop. I came across an interesting concept that might apply: purity. Not just innocence, in that time frame, but also a further, fuzzier meaning that is hard to describe. I don't think

The only negative aspect I can't escape, as the days roll by in comfort, is that the cha have quite a strong smell. But it turns out that smell is relative. A person can only smell of cha if there's another person there to comment on it, and pretty soon I'm comfortable with the idea that I've come to smell like a cha, and they have maybe got used to my smell. I'm assuming I also have a smell.

We all relax together in the hot tub in the evening, and although the tub is therefore very crowded and very hairy, it's still fun.

But every afternoon the cha leave, and they return in the evening. Where do they go? I want to know. I need to know.

381

I FOLLOW THEM, and they return to the slopes of the mountain, close to the road. There they spend their time nibbling grass and playing little cha games, hopping over and around each other.

'Are you waiting for questers?' I ask them. They don't reply—they are just animals—but something in their manner makes me think I'm right. And that is lovely.

---

they were ever considered 'peak pure' (cyber language: a dark forest of meaning) as they do not dominate cyber culture. For further discussion see *We Can Haz Emotional Significance* by FRGJ CHG (RAB39335558).

They really are looking out for the best interests of questers. But what happens when another quester comes along? Will I be expected to leave?

There are four bedrooms, I tell myself, as I return to the chalet. The thought of sharing the place, even though there is easily room for more, bothers me. The hair and the smell. There would have to be a human judgement applied to these things. No more sleeping and hot tubbing with cha, perhaps. No more being one of them.

Still, the days pass and nobody else comes.

Until there is a day when the cha don't come back at all.

The afternoon passes into the evening and none of my little friends appear. I make my own light salad. I can't face hot tubbing without their company, so in the last light of the day I set off down the slope, back along the road, to find them. Instead I find, right at the spot where I first set eyes on them, blood spattered through the tough grass, red fur in chunks. I collect up the dripping pieces and it's not even enough to make one cha.

The blood is plenteous, the most I've ever seen. It coats this quiet place, paints it with a terrible menace I didn't see before. I would call out for the cha—are they hiding? could some of them have escaped?—but I can't find my voice and I slink away, back to the chalet.

I bury the pieces of not even one whole cha by the back door, around the corner from the hot tub, and I say a few words:

Thank you for helping me
I'm so sorry this happened to you
I don't understand this world[33]

I go back inside, my face aching from crying, and I lie awake, listening for a murderer. Or the breathing man. Or one and the same.

---

33 Contrary to what Fairly thinks here, I don't really think it would have been a surprise to the reader in any preceding human age that cute/pure creatures die horribly in both fictions and in the real world. Animal cruelty was abolished globally in 2203 following scientific advancement in agriculture/growth culture that revolutionised farming techniques and, together with capture tech and organic replenishment, began the land reclamation projects that opened the gateway to the reformation of nation states. Before that, only the truly sheltered (further study in variations of richness VOR45938058) could have claimed to be unaware of mass animal abuse. 'History is the greatest horror' – The Vampire Reclamation Project VRP49670076. (It's a great quote, but I wouldn't advise getting too close to the VRP unless you like bite marks on your body. Having an organic form can create all sorts of weird urges, sometimes.)

Current organic life laws allow projects of genetic reclamation to take place – but only for those animals who can be successfully incorporated into existing reserves without compromising their instincts/behaviours. This means I may never see a world with a totally 'free' Bengal tiger or great white shark. This remains a source of constant friction addressed by the spire-based streams. The dialogue continues.

381

THE MORNING COMES around, and none of the cha have returned.

Nothing has come for me. There is relief in that, and in every minute that passes and takes me further away from the blood on the grass. I keep the doors shut and the long windows locked up tight.

The house just isn't the same without the cha.

I wander idly through the rooms, touching the décor that now feels emptied of emotion. I wonder if it was designed only to please questers, in an objective style. Am I like other questers? I open all the cupboards and closets, looking for evidence of what cha like, how cha live. Everything is empty. In a small pantry jutting off from the kitchen I find a half-size door, stiff to open, and beyond it there is a library. Huge. Too big for the dimensions of the house, even—a magical collection of reading material, and every book I pick up is about cha. Who knew so many books existed on the subject? It's astonishing. I browse cha care, cha husbandry, cha wifedom, cha kids. There's a whole shelf of fairy tales: three tiny cha, the cha prince. In some versions a cha becomes famous, or rich, or gets married to a beautiful woman. I didn't realise cha wanted to marry humans. No wonder they help us, open up their houses to us. Perhaps they were watching me undress every night. Perhaps they were filming it, with a peephole in the ceiling or a two-way mirror with a camera sitting behind it. My whole experience of cha generosity is being cheapened. It's not straightforward, after all.

The more I read, the more I get the impression that these books weren't even written by humans. They read as if cha wrote them. That fundamentally changes my thoughts about them. Are they as complex as humans? Did I assume that some human, somewhere, was in charge of all the cha, controlling their actions? How, exactly, do their lives intersect with ours? I was disrespectful of their autonomy. *How cute*: I thought. There's so much more to it than that. I wish they would come back, so I could try to understand them better. But they're gone, I think, and the blood returns to my mind.

381

I FIND A book in the cha library about questers.

THE GREAT CHA QUEST PROPHECY
HANDBOOK[34]

---

34 I can't find this document. Plus, the ridiculousness of looking at some dodgy old document to try to find personal answers! (Forgive a joke at my own expense there.) This library (as a physical representation of

I take the book up to the bedroom I picked, lie out on the bed, and read it from cover to cover. I picture the unseen camera filming me, catching me in this act.

It's not a book about quests.

It's about how to prophesy for humans who are on quests and who might happen to need a break, just off the horned road, because they're imminently approaching an important life realisation, or ILR.

The book doesn't say what the ILR might be.

The actual business of prophesying is a banal one: twitching, hopping, licking, making small furry noises. All of these actions are meant to open humans up to cosmic vibes that explain the path ahead, on some level. It didn't work at all for me. I feel no closer to understanding any of it. But the existence of the book, the fact that cha train for this purpose: that is incredibly reassuring. It's a revelation. I have, despite my meanderings and panics and general lack of knowledge and confidence so far, ended up in the right place. This is all working out.

Until the cha got attacked.

If that's what happened.

Or maybe this is part of their prophecy. I reread the book, carefully, but nothing mentions staging a massacre

knowledge deemed unknowable) embodies the Magical Manifestation of Knowledge theory expounded by DR Fedlow in *What Book? Where?* (MMK29555960).

and then hiding. No, I'm certain they meant to still be here, twitching and tubbing and trying to lead my thoughts in certain directions. Surely there are more of them out there? Even one survivor would be enough. With this thought in my mind, I head back out to the slopes and look around, look hard. I spend hours hoping to catch sight of one.

Nothing.

And it comes to me that I can't wait for them to provide the answers anyway. Even if they did return, I didn't get their message. I might as well push on, and hope to see other cha, make other connections.

I make a light salad in loneliness, and I eat. I take one more hairy dip in the hot tub. I sleep. In the morning I leave the chalet, slipping the key under the pot, and I put my feet on the horned road once more.

381

BACK TO THE mountain with teeth! Yes. Enough of cha tragedy and time-wasting. I need to look up, look onwards, past the pool and the library and tasteful furniture. With the rucksack on my back, my water bottle filled, I tackle the incline.

Higher and higher, up into the great light that breaks through the clouds, vast billowing, moving fast, illuminating a view to die for, the towering rocks. The path narrows, threatens to peter out, so I feel I'm almost lost, but there's always a trace underfoot, through pasture, over boulders. The road returns. Or is it still the same road? A new journey? Every single time? If a break in continuation is the end, then I am being filled and blessed by so many new beginnings. But then I remember: night and day, the episodic nature of the journey, of this life. That's it. This life is the continuation. Not the road. Not the cha. Not the breathing man, who comes and goes and lurks and is maybe behind me or maybe in front of me.

The mountain of teeth rises higher, and this evening there will be only the tent, the sleeping bag. I'm open to the elements. Oh, for a door and a key. For cha to keep me safe. Is that what they were doing? Yes, they were keeping me safe.

It's so cold up here, and the air is thin in my throat. The few remaining plants—hardy looking scrubs and brushes, and the occasional glimpse of a tiny white flower face—are welcome diversions from the rock, and from nowhere I find there is a sudden drop to the ground far below on either side; the path feels unsure to me, suspended, like a walkway. Finding a stretch of toughened, hardy grass a little further on is a relief.

I set up the tent and lie inside, feeling the dark.

The walls are a kind of protection, it's true, but it's an illusion of solidity. Although—wasn't the house much the same? If something terrible had wanted in, would anything have stopped it?

And I'm at the whim of the world, and anything else is not true. I wonder if this is a quest for truth. If so, perhaps I'm already doing well.

381

I'M IN THE dark again.

Outside dark is so much darker than inside dark.

I miss the chalet.

Maybe the cha have returned now. Maybe their disappearance was their way of telling me that my time in their hospitality, eating their salads and so on, was up. They faked their own deaths. But the blood was so real. Would I have known if it was fresh, real blood? I've never even seen much of my own blood. I am so inexperienced that I can't even tell if I've seen a real massacre or not. How does a person tell the difference?

Does it matter either way? No, I reason, as I probably won't ever see them again. Not that bunch of cha, anyway. So I'll choose to imagine them alive, and sneaking back to the key under the pot, and giving the hot tub a quick clean out ready for the next quester.

The thought of the hot tub, fresh bubbling water over energised, fizzing skin, inspires the strong desire to pee.

So I leave the relative safety of the sleeping bag, the tent, and out on the mountain of teeth I go, squatting near a small and beleaguered shrub. The darkness is not so absolute, and not so conducive to making up my own reality. There are moments in which the lighter and brighter darknesses clash to create shapes that might even coalesce into forms.

Is that him?

I am peeing, I can't stop. I have to bear the trickle of the flow, and it is so loud that I am certain his ears are attuned to it, and this is the most defenceless, vulnerable, I have ever been. I can't stand tall, I can't move. I am an animal, caught in the body's demands, unable to control them. I am a baby again. I will be killed. I will be eaten. The mountain has teeth. I don't want to be eaten after all.

Done.

I scramble to pull up my trousers, return to the tent, and curl up in the bag.

If it had been the breathing man, he could have killed me right there.

I'm at the whim of the world, my brain says all night, and I listen to it carefully. It says a lot of things.

IT SAYS THINGS like:

I am not a dreamer. I am not caught up in circumstances created purely by my own imagination. I am not immune to my imagination, but I am not in the thrall of what my mind creates, and this ground is real, this cold slice of night running through the tent is real. I am not utterly empty. I am here now, and the events happening to me are filling me up, heavy and weighty. I am not without meaning, or free of time and distance. I have travelled for many days already, a certain amount of miles, and that creates its own purpose. I will continue to speak to myself while this night goes on, but there will be a morning and there will be movement, and he is not here, not outside, not now. Who knows where he is? No. Don't think that, that doesn't help. A huge world and he could fill it, be everywhere, if I think him into every corner of every crack of every space. I don't want to get hurt, or damaged. That's natural. The basic starting point of any adventure is not to be hurt, not permanently, not in a way that doesn't force me to grow, to blossom, to overcome. I don't think I have been hurt in either way yet. Does that mean I'm still at the beginning of this story? My own first words: *Don't hurt me*. The people in my village talk about how quests aren't what they used to be, but I think the same thing has probably hidden at the heart of every quester through time—the avoidance of pain. Later, we might learn to share, or to blame, in plural. The giant *We did it this way and you lot want it all like this*. Deep inside, it all feels the same. I want to believe that. Journeys don't change. The night is letting go. My brain is loosening its grip. I am not a dreamer and here comes the morning to get me. Wake up, get up, pack up the tent. Tell the body to move. If I am not the brain and not the body, what am I? I don't know what I am. But I am not a dreamer.[35]

381

THE FINAL ASCENT to the top of the mountain of teeth is treacherous, exposed, the wind strong in my face and

---

35 At this moment Fairly sounds like a lecturer I had in my second year of Curation, as part of socialisation. I would have been fifteen, in organic years? 'Stop dreaming of a better world,' he said to me, when checking my early attempts at understanding documents of the past (I had the bad habit of looking for ways we could take ideas to apply them to our future). 'We're already in the better world, as long as you realise that's what it is. When you aim higher, you lower the ground you stand on.' If Fairly does not dream, then she will not strive. That's right: she's definitely telling lies. Her unreliability established, how can we believe a word she writes? (Further question for consideration: does that matter? I have no idea what I'm doing. What am I doing?)

the ground slippery. But it is not a climb. At no point do I scale rocks. The road becomes clearer at this point. I am in no doubt, this morning at least, that I'm going in the right direction.

The road levels out and I find, surprisingly, that there is no more up before the down. I would have liked it to be more demanding at its pinnacle. Then this view, over a land, over fields and houses—Telezon behind me, and ahead the sea—would have felt like an earned achievement, and I would have looked at it through different eyes, conquering eyes. Instead I'm looking down as a tourist. I own nothing. It gives me nothing. There are other tourists up here. They're milling about, taking photographs. A cable car drop-off point is close by, for those who are not on quests.

There's a squat brown signpost that reads:

CAVE OF TEETH

It's followed by an arrow, so I walk in the direction indicated and find, on this bright morning, a small ticket booth. As the cable cars arrive the tourists seethe out of the retracting doors and slide along to form a queue, where they have conversations, leaning into the booth, flashing cards, then head into an area demarcated by metal poles and yellow tape.

I join the queue. I do not make eye contact with the

person in the booth, and simply tag along, on the back of a wedge of tourists. Nobody shouts, nobody complains. Can't they see I'm not one of their number? They swallow me up. Perhaps this is what that boy meant, back at the bottom.

Maybe I don't want to be swallowed up by a group like this. Not forever. But there's something about tagging along, being part of their number, that is good right now. Their conversations spread over me like a canopy. They talk about the weather, the cable car, the things they are hoping to see. They are excitable yet banal, and I find pride in my status as quester. I'm not one of them. Why, then, am I pretending to be?

A bigger sign:

CAVE OF TEETH

381

I AM AT a majestic opening, rising from the ground, invading the sky. It's a hole that leads down into the inner workings of the mountain, and the shape is a pleasing oval rimmed with whiter, smaller rocks that jut up, hang down, in broken lines. Stalactites and stalagmites.

It is a mouth. The mouth of the mountain.

I definitely don't want to be swallowed, after all.

I hang back, but the crowd of tourists carries me in.

They have no issues. They take photographs, and point, and exclaim. They and I make a *we*, and we enter the maw. We are being fed to the mountain. We will not emerge, will we? I shudder, walking over the threshold. It feels like an important moment.

But once we're in it's not so bad.[36]

In fact, it's pretty standard, as impressive natural wonders go. The jutting rocks are charismatic at first, but soon fade from interesting to tripping hazards. There's some fun to be had in calling out *echo, echo, echooooo* for a while, and then my crowd of tourists stops playing that game and moves on, and I find myself feeling alone once more.

There's a kiosk a hundred yards away, near one of the biggest stalagmites. The side of the kiosk leans against it at an angle. Two women are turning meat on a spit, over coals. There is no flame or smoke, but as I get closer I can feel great heat emanating from it. I don't understand how it works.

The meat, packaged into small round bundles placed along the spit, sizzles. It smells of good times and victory, and celebration.

---

36 I am deep inside the story, too; is this the true moment of no return? Even if she was to turn around right now and march back, putting her feet precisely where she walked, she would be a different person upon her arrival. And even if I stop this personal project now, I will still be altered by this narrative. Nothing seems quite so solid anymore. I'm different, she's different. We are linked!

'One in a bun?' says one of the women—the woman not turning the spit handle right now. They are both dressed in some sort of costume that comes with tassels, lace, and large pointed shoes with curving toes.

'What is it?' I ask.

'Local delicacy.'

I look hard at the meat. I see the arched back, the tucked legs. The triangular ears.

'No,' I say. 'No, I don't want any.' The smell makes me both hungry and human. When I turn around, the mouth of the cave is looming above me, white teeth snapping, and I am swallowed by my self-disgust without any fight at all.

381

Is THIS WHAT humanity does? We take those who help us and turn them into products to be devoured?

I am blinded, deafened. There is a scratching sound close by, then a soft roar of deep, warm wind swells up, pulls my hair, dries the sudden tears on my face. I return to the stand and I smell the food, the food overwhelms everything. I have to be alive, even if others are dead. Even more so, *because* they are dead.

I think this means I have a new responsibility.

'How much?' I ask the women, and the one turning the handle says, 'A cha.' She says it without irony. That is the price.

I take out my cha and hold them in my hand, the two of them. I know this is the right thing to do. I give her one of my cha. She takes it and pockets it in the deep fold at the front of her pinafore. Then she lifts the handle and slides the charred corpse from the spit. She wraps it in paper and hands it to me with ceremony. The trade has been made.

I juggle it to unwrap it, one hot hand to another, and I reveal one small amount to the elements, to my eyes. It is meat. I lift it to my mouth, and I bite. The heat holds for a moment, then mellows, and it is soft and giving, releasing flavour, and I want more, I dig in. I separate the flesh from the bones and make a meal of my little saviour. I do not feel shame. I feel closer to them.

'Good, right?' says the woman by the spit, and the other says, with such pride, 'The best.'

There's a bin beside the spit. I deposit the bones and the paper, and I wonder: what is this quest? It is changing. I feel it inside me, catch the act of metamorphosis with a side-order of amnesia—it is a monster, this quest. It is a million different metaphors.

I look around and see the tourists have moved further into the cave, so I hurry to catch up with them. I want to be with them. I want a sense of direction, and they all seem to have one.

381

I JOIN THE back of their number. They have moved through to a smaller cave that slopes away underfoot and crumbles. The lighting is dimmer, and the stalactites and -mites even larger. The tourists break apart, exclaim over these pointed teeth, lift up their cameras, and aim, and snap. 'Look at the point on this one!' says a voice with an accent I don't recognise, all drawl, and the tourists swing as one to the spot, and collect upon it. Then they part, scatter with their lenses blinking, and return to their random darting. I feel grateful for them, shining their lights, their eyes, so randomly. Their directions can be my directions for a while. When they move further down again, into the real dark, I keep pace. The flashes of their cameras[37] are moments in my story.

Flash one: I am illuminated.

---

37 Mechanisms of illumination once more – how could she have such faith in devices? How can she find faith in anything? How on earth does a person live in that time and space, in conflict, in loneliness, in pain? I can only look back at that time and wonder. The process of understanding the Age of Riches is, I fear, beyond us all, because we will never know what it feels like to be the epicentre of an ocean in turmoil, unable to reach higher ground, unable to find any perspective on that experience.

Can any time know another?

If not, what is the point of history?

Flash two: I am grateful.

Flash three: I am among them.

Flash four: I move in time.

Flash five: Further in, further down, and on in further flashes, further flashes.

We go on that way for what feels like miles, until my eyes are so tired of their lights, and I begin to feel shame at the never-ending nature of them. People are such hard work, aren't they? They don't pause and they don't delineate. Each flash is as good as the next, but no learning is taking place; nobody is saying, *This is better than the last,* or, *I'm beginning to understand this place.*

So is this what humanity is, then? A group of beings who don't belong anywhere, muscling in and snapping their seconds away? From the depth of this cave of teeth to the tip of the Spire of Telezon, they have infiltrated. And I wanted to be one of them. Is this a quest, or a holiday? Is this meaning, or just making time pass?

A girl is at my side.

She is half my size, and I would guess maybe half my age. She is peering at me through the dark, and I watch as her hand slides into mine. I feel it, hard and hot, and then the comfort of it slips away again and in the next flash she is staring at me as if she doesn't know me at all.

'WHERE ARE YOU from?' says the girl. 'Do you live here? In the cave?'

'No, I'm just visiting,' I tell her, and she shakes her head at me and says, 'I thought you didn't look like us. I live here.' She is proud of that apparent fact, although I doubt its truth. Her accent matches the voice from earlier. That drawl, as if from far away.

'Tam!' calls a voice, booming, or perhaps that's not the word at all. Perhaps its Jam. Or Sam. Or Pam. Some name like the clang of a musical instrument on a hard surface, or the dentist tapping my teeth. Teeth everywhere. Cave of teeth, mouth of teeth, and I'm no closer to understanding any of it. What is humanity? Why do I care? I want to unpack the journey, the life, the anything, and the girl grabs my hand, and then there is a roaring, like a lion, everything here is just like something else. A roaring lion, so loud, and somebody screams just as water arrives, a vast cascade of it, suddenly upon me; it spews up from the ground, rushing around the stalagmites, and it is soaking all of us, this dirty icy water.

This is it, this is the end, this is me dead. I am flailing, the water is already ankle deep. The girl clings to me and I let go, shake her off. She moves away, falls down, and I see the water carry her away, and then the ground is no longer solid and the water is up to my hips, and my trousers are a heavy second skin. There's a current, strong, that hits the back of my knees. I fall down, can't catch my breath in the cold. It wants to take me with it. I am being moved, an object, I can't find anything to stop this progress down further, further, the water has a path into the greatest depths of the cave. I am slipping, being swallowed—yes! This is the swallowing. The dark is complete. I can't breathe. Pain in my leg, my head. Rocks. Water. This is me dead. No, this is me alive.

I am alive.

I wake on a beach, in sunshine, and soft music is playing from some place close by.

381

I TURN MY hurting head from side to side on the sand, but the music is not coming from any one direction. It's not locatable. It's soft, loud, all tinnitus and distant drums. It's easy listening and nagging doubt. It's in my head, I realise, crystallise it: *It's in my head*. I'm alone, with only music for company, and it's a tune I've never heard before.

My clothes are a horrible embrace. Clammy. I make myself stand, stagger away from the mouth of the cave and the river that flows from it. Tall, thick trees with verdant green leaves are all around. A turtle is watching me from a sandflat in centre of the river, its head tilted in my direction. I call out to it, a *hello*, and it does not reply.

Is this turtle my new best friend? My ally? Am I to live here, now, until the end of my days, with this turtle for company?[38] But no, no, it's moving itself from the sandbank on its clumsy flippers, and then it dives and it's gone. The music intensifies, a swell of sadness, and I am naked, uncomfortable, but also I am myself again. I pick the pieces of myself up, feel around my throbbing head wound with my fingers, and a voice calls out, 'Jam!' or perhaps it is Ham or Clam. The girl. The girl, I remember her, the voice is calling her. A small group of bedraggled tourists emerges from the rocks, their eyes searching in all directions. They see me, wave at me. They come over to me. One of them is holding my backpack; I take it from his outstretched hands and he says, 'Have you seen a little girl?'

The music in my head shuts off.

I put on the backpack. It's heavier than ever before, waterlogged, and I say, 'No.'

---

38 Shipwreck/abandonment documents cross fact/fiction, engaging imagination freely – creating both apprehension and desire (SHW33049508).

And guilt. Guilt. How will she live with it? She'll move. Maybe that's what journeys are for. To move away from the person you were when you were standing still.

No, I haven't seen her since I let her go.

'Let's keep looking,' says a woman, and the man says to me, 'Help us, come with us, we're all going to stick together until help arrives.'

I don't want to help, or to be helped. I want to get as far away from all these feelings as possible. I shake my head, and he frowns, and he leaves with the others.

381

DO WE ALWAYS emerge from caves? Is that the law?

I start walking in the opposite direction, following the river, and I find a small sign at the start of the trees that reads:

EVERYONE WHO ENTERS MUST LEAVE:
HURRY ONWARDS RIGHT NOW
NOT IN THE FUTURE

Is that meant to be deep, philosophical? I'm in no mood for that, having discovered I don't like the music that plays inside me. Perhaps the sign is specific to questers who sneak inside, and emerge in bright sunlight, and decide to go no further. Maybe there are legions of us. Maybe we've formed a community, separate from and disdainful of the tourists. We gather mushrooms and other slimy things to eat, we drink of the cold river water, we make home brew from squeezed rocks and homespun wisdom. I head into the forest. I'm almost certain that, really, there isn't a group of us in here.

But there is a path.

Is it my path?

The sign. *Hurry onwards, right now.*

H.O.R.N.

This is the horned road.[39] I'm certain of it. Hurry onwards, yes. I will. I will.

As I walk, overhead branches obscure the sun and briars snatch at my still damp trousers, but I have the strongest feeling that the road will keep me safe, even if it is getting dark. Or is that just the forest closing over me? It doesn't matter either way. I have my backpack. I have the will to continue.

And the road leads me away, and then it curves to the left and there, in a clearing, is a horse and cart with a blue cross painted on a banner attached to one side.

The driver is young, attractive, a little older than me. Old enough to be a man, not a boy. He sees me, and nods without much interest. 'We heard there was an emergency,' he says.

---

39 As mentioned in my introduction, puzzles/codes feature in the document in numerous ways, both for Fairly to solve, and – I think – for me to solve. But I can't, I can't, I'm not up to this task. I never should have started it. I'm trapped.

'It's not me,' I tell him. 'A little girl was swept away. They're looking for her.' I point back over my shoulder.[40]

'Swept away?'

'There was a flood.'

That seems to make up his mind. He picks up a plastic case from the seat beside him, hops down from the cart, and heads in the direction of the cave.

I am left alone with the horse.

381

A HORSE CAN be many things.

It can be a servant, an animal, a friend, a freedom.

Right now, what is this horse?

I'm not afraid of horses, but I do have horse baggage. When I was younger, nine or ten, my friend Cecile liked horses and chose a day out riding for her birthday party. Suitably kitted out, we all took it in turns to ride a little pony. I was the smallest and my legs could barely fit around its bulk. It was a shock, that barrel middle. Even little ponies are big to little girls. The pony was not at all interested in any of us, I don't think, but it was obedient

---

40 She was swept away because of Fairly!

I already know she's a liar. I wonder if she really can find herself, or lead me to any real answers. If she can't admit responsibility for anything, how can I allow her to be responsible for helping me?

in a resigned way, until it saw a good patch of grass on the far side of a low fence, and took it into its hooves to get there.

It was inconsequential, just a removal of the notion that I was ever in control of it, perched high up there with my legs out sideways. No, it was always in control of me, and it ignored me beautifully as it jumped the fence and ate the grass. Eventually it finished its meal and looked around at me. *You still here?*

End of story.

Did all my big life events take place during birthday parties?

All horses are a pretence of subservience laid over apparent cooperation: that's my theory, anyway. Why do they pretend to cooperate? For food? For an easy life?

Come to think of it, why am I cooperating?

For food.

For an easy life.

Yes, I'm a cooperator. A collaborator. A wet one, drowned in my own belief in the quest, the hero, the meaning of absolutely fucking[41] everything like the worst

---

41 A 'rude' word. It's a bit of a shock to come across one here, only because that doesn't fit how I was thinking of Fairly (but I was wrong! I will admit it, even if she won't). Why does she use it now? It feels like a call to action.

Some historical context via the stream: The concept of some words being unacceptable in certain company

kind of enabler. I am my own enabler.

I move to the horse and stroke its nose.

Meanwhile, people are having problems everywhere.

A handsome young man is trying to help a group of tourists to find a child that I shook off like an annoyance because she just wasn't as important as me. I'm having a lot of personal revelations in front of this horse.

I could steal it. Mount it, make like a picture of escape, and ride far away.

Let's face it, I'm not going to do that.

381

PEOPLE. PROBLEMS. EVERYWHERE.

Not just the missing child. All over the world.

---

has been argued to stem from the use of language as a gatekeeping device/social stricture. As communication technology advanced and the est. 7,100 languages in daily use around the world in that age began to freely mingle and evolve, the explosion of 'rude' words eventually rendered the concept obsolete. Bluntly put, 'rude' words were a victim of their own success. Mjoubi argues that the decline of the idea of the unsayable impacts upon the idea of the undoable, eroding both, until rudimentary moral library management via the Magnaman method begins to separate the concepts at the end of the age (FUK01002301).

The stream misses something I have found. Rude words still work! Weird.

But at least I have this horned road to follow.

So I follow it. I leave the horse with a fond pat and start walking again, and I camp when the sun goes down and I move when the sun comes up, and I see nothing and nobody that should not be there as I traverse the charming forest, and every day I put that little girl (who probably drowned) out of my mind a little more. It's not easy, but it is possible. It's possible to live as if the journey is the most important thing in the world, and to justify all happenings in that belief. I'm grateful for it.

The forest dwindles to dirt, and the road widens. My feet are toughened, my back strong. I'm hardened in new ways. I reach a coast again, a sea wall built of boulders on my left, and an unnamed ocean beyond it. A few houses, and the locals come out to curtsey or bow as I pass. They know about questers, it seems. I take their gifts of milk and bread, and I bow back. Then: a wall.

It's a wall like the one around my hometown, and I feel weepy for a moment. The road leads through a large gate, past the wall, and inside there's a wooden sign:

DISTRACTION

Underneath it is written a whole lot of information about the town. Such as the fact that the wall is ornamental only. The people who were there before the current people built it, and then the current people came and found the wall didn't keep them out in the least, but they could appreciate it represented a whole lot of hard work, which made it attractive in its own way, and also handy for hanging the dead bodies of the people who were there before the current people. But that was all a long time ago.[42]

I leave the sign, and bow and curtsey my way around the current people. The wall, and the road, curves around to the rocks of a clean blue bay, like a postcard picture. There's a bigger gate there, which is shut very firmly, with an air of finality about it.

381

I KNOCK ON the gate. I knock for a while, until it becomes obvious, even to me, that nobody is going to answer, and it reminds me of the time I hesitated outside a door, as a child, at a birthday party[43], full of nerves about whether

---

42 How wonderful it must have been to live in a time when a group consensus existed about history, rather than a hole that we try to fill with the things we think we understand. It was an illusion, no doubt, but a good and comforting one.

43 Another birthday party moment! Fairly's life exists in segmentation. 381 words, section after section, month after month, birthday after birthday. I can identify with her, here. The recent global accord to abandon longevity treatments in favour of quality of life initiatives means that

the party would be in full swing on the other side of the door. And then I heard someone, a popular someone, possibly Cecile, say:

Fairly is just weird, isn't she?

I ended up not going through that door, but waiting out in the garden for the party to come to me, smile in place. But that makes me even more determined to make it through this gate so I knock louder, louder, until someone nervous comes hurrying up and says, 'It's open, it's open for questers, just go on through, dear.' I push, and the door just opens. It's like magic. It gives in to me so easily, and I thank the nervous person, and bow, and behind it is an even bigger town with a wooden sign that reads:

INTERVENTION

---

the body must cease on its seventieth birthday. There is seen to be no perceived benefit to consciousness enclosed in ailing flesh – but what about what suffering can teach us? Surely it has meaning.

Personally, I voted against this accord, and have therefore been offered a place in a Negatory Tract. I don't think I want to take it up. Why reject everything about this society that works on the basis of one held belief? Besides, I should make more of my organic life. I should. I know I should. Sitting here working on this document night and day: I'm missing so many opportunities to move.

But nobody seems to live in this town.[44]

The street leading to the centre is empty, the houses crowded around it silent and watchful.

How can a whole townsfolk beyond a townsfolk have disappeared?

I enter, and the nervous person closes the gate behind me, and I am alone. I walk the street, reach the main square, see a fountain of roughly carved cherubs spurting water, and the trickling sound is pleasant, but loud, too loud in the absence of other sounds. Human noises are needed. I notice how everything is in order, and I know how unnatural that is.

In the absence of company, stimulation—without the widening of a personality that comes as a response to the rough little abrasions, the cuts and scratches of interaction—how does a person move on?

I sit by the fountain. I expect, at first, that I'll relax into this emptiness.

The longer it goes on, the less relaxed I feel.

There's nobody here, I tell myself. *Relax, relax.*

---

44 Again, no evidence of either of these towns existing in reality. Are locations real until we visit them? Does a tree fall in the woods etc? Thanks, ancient scholars, for pointing out that nothing has ever seemed quite real to anyone. At least I'm not alone in that. Last night a crow tapped on my window, like an omen, like a… signpost. I thought it was the breathing man. A change is coming. I can't escape it.

All my senses sharpen.

I tell myself, *This is ridiculous,* and I stand, pick a house at random, and knock, and enter, and each empty room, blank window, makes it worse.

Hello, I call. *Hello.*

381

THERE ARE UNPACKED suitcases on top of unemptied wardrobes in every single bedroom where I sleep, and I spend many nights here because I cannot move on without answers. Why does this place stand? Why would everybody leave it behind? It's crazy to care, I know that. Perhaps it's the job of a hero to investigate all small variations in the pattern. I wish I didn't feel that way. I put my feet to the road every day, and reach the outskirts of Intervention, but then I turn around and choose another bedroom for another night.

The kitchens have stocked cupboards. The inn has a working jukebox, and I choose a song and press the flashing button, desperate for friendly voices, but the song is so loud I clap my hands to my ears and howl, like a dog, like a protest at loneliness, as a band sings *together, forever, love, love, love, love* and other assorted words.

These townsfolk all left together without taking anything. Or maybe they were the things that were taken. Somebody took them. Who takes people away? Only spacecraft and monsters.

Just thinking about monsters brings me back to the memory of my breathing man.

Where is he? It's an age since I've seen him. Have I left him behind?

I use my new trick and decide to stop thinking about the thing that bothers me, so I push the thought of monsters to the back. Perhaps this is a relocation plan—an entire town, moved on. If so, there'll be official documents.

I leave the pub and search for a council building. I know what they look like, and I find it pretty quickly. It's just like the one in my village, with a sloping roof and portico, backed up against the wall. The double doors are unlocked, like every other door in town. The framed photographs in the reception area show a succession of historical mayors in finery, the same weighty chain around each neck, the smile above it always a little nervy, unsure.

The portraits are the only example of humanity I find. This place is empty, too, but there is a note left, pinned to a cork noticeboard amid declarations of sports days and missing pets and a jam-making course on Saturdays:

381

EVENT SCHEDULED

it says.

ALL WELCOME FOR WORLD CLASS
HIDE AND SEEK INSTRUCTION FOLLOWED BY
A BID TO BREAK THE WORLD RECORD!
SPEAK TO:

And then a name. A date that might be this date.

I remember hide and seek. I never liked it, but I was good at it. The hiding part, at least. Alone in dark shadows, not breathing in plain sight, just tucked behind a door. One time I curled up behind the stove, uncomfortably warm; thank goodness nobody stoked it. The longer the game goes on, the worse it gets—that feeling of imminent discovery. A looming face. *Found you!* I don't remember ever being caught. Only the feeling of it remains. I wonder if I used to pre-empt that moment, and emerge, and call out: *Here I am!* Just to wriggle free from the expectation[45].

---

45 I used to play hide and seek too, at socialisation. We were all encouraged to get to know our bodies and their capabilities, and part of that involved time spent just running around and playing physical games. It satisfies

I walk out of the town hall and stand in the square. I call out:

Here I am.

Nothing moves.

The feeling is so unbearable that I have to make it clear that I am refusing to play. I run from the town, freed from the spell to remain. I get as far away as I can that day, and I file Intervention as one more place I never want to think about again.

The longer I run the less landscape there is.

At first I blame the weather. This must be a fog. But I can't see fog; does that make sense? Surely I could see fog if it was there. There must be something wrong with my eyes. Have I aged that much? I feel I've hardly aged at all. This should be a journey that belongs to youth, and apparently I'm aging all the time. It's unfair. It's unhelpful. Soon all my energy and optimism will be a

---

both growing body and mind. For the mind is a growth process too – the human/streaming synthesis taught us that. A stream placed in a baby's body leads to no division between them in the formation of consciousness. To put it simply – I am not a 'we'. I am just 'me'. The stream inside me has had previous experiences in bodies, under different names, just as the flesh had direct descendants. Those people are not me either. We grow into our own forms, every time.

Some things remain; they outlast time. And some things cannot be outrun.

thing of the past, and the only thing I can still see is the sea, still on my left, blue in a world of grey.

No. No, I'm crying. That's all that's wrong. That's nothing at all.

I stop running, and control myself. My eyes eventually obey. How long and straight the road is! Only the faintest of lines delineates it from the landscape, and it all fades to one in the distance, and goes nowhere. So I sit down.

381

I LOOK AT my own hands and see the flesh so vivid, like a cartoon character drawn on paper, coloured in. There is artifice to my hands. I put them on my chest, feel my heartbeat through my sturdy, comfortable clothing.

I'm not certain I'm real.

I set up my tent and I stay at that spot, uncoloured, undefined, for a length of time. I can't say how long. But there's no point to that protest either, and the more I stay still the more I expect the breathing man to arrive.

So I get up, pack up, and start walking again.

At least the act of walking is always reassuring.

It goes on and on.

Eventually my supplies start to run low. What I wouldn't give for a bowing or curtseying local with a gift in their hands. I can't tell what season it is, and nothing grows here.

I eke out what I have, and I live with hunger.

Then it comes to me that I am walking uphill. The slope is too gradual to notice, at first, but then it becomes more definite, and then turns positively challenging. Uphill again. It both cheers and depresses me. A new adventure that feels an awful lot like the ones I've had before.

It becomes another destination to reach on this quest, and reach it I do.

At the top of this hill there sits a chain device.

It's exactly like the one that started my quest.

It's a large metal cube, smooth sides, topped with a button. It has been fixed in place, the grass on the tump it stands upon growing up around the sides. It has been there for some time. It looks a little rusted by the salt from the sea, giving it a greenish quality. Because it has a view out over the sea, so blue, and the grey has dissipated to give me a beautiful view and a bath of sunshine on my skin, which feels real to me again. Colour. I am real. This is real. It is spring. I know it in my bones. I will see flowers and taste fruits.

My relief is so strong as to be joy, and as I examine the device I realise I'm in a good mood.

381

THE DEVICE IS similar to the one in the town hall at home, and also different.

The marks of heavy use upon it, the scratches on the sides, the rusting, reminds me of the rotavator they used to have at the farm along the way from my mother's house. This is an object that works hard.

I look around for instructions. Or for some sign of recognition, of praise, for making it this far—isn't it an achievement? Haven't I travelled farther than others? But I see nothing. There is the button, of course. Just like before. I must push the button. Am I brave enough to push the button?

Not quite yet. But I am brave enough to touch it. To lay a hand on it. And the contact is reassuring. It is a warm device; it has soaked up the sunshine too. The one in the departure lounge back home was cold.

Go on, then.

I tell myself.

Go on.

I try to push it and it won't move at first, and then. And then. It gives, a little, and gives, a bit more, and then it depresses, fully in, and at first nothing is different. The device is the same, except—yes, a small flap has opened quietly, without fanfare, at knee level. You would have missed it but[46] it banged against your skin when you

---

46 Would you have missed it? It leads the way into the next section of the document in which Fairly moves into an even more surreal realm. This next part reads to me like a nightmare. Unnumbered, uncontrolled.

shifted your weight as if it wanted to be noticed. You crouch down, rubbing your knee, and see a pamphlet protruding from the flap. You pull it free. It comes with reluctance. You read the first paragraph:

Congratulations on your purchase of the Chain Device 2.0! With a lifetime of good management and proper care the Chain Device can illuminate generations of questers during their sifting process, providing all the knowledge they need to complete their journeys with maximum efficiency and only minimal discomfort. Your purchase entitles you to regular servicing that will be provided by the Care and Hospitality Association, to be arranged through the helpline number 381.

The pamphlet is snatched from your hand by the wind, and you look up, realise the good weather has already left you and the light is fading. The sky is dark, silver clouds gather, and how different it all looks now. How portentous.

381

AND YOU FEEL it—he is here. You know it before he crests the hill. The black hair, the broad shoulders, the drive of those lean legs. He is here, and he was never very far behind, not really. How far you thought you came—and at times you even forgot about him, but that was your own self-interest at work, allowing you to pretend you were the centre of the world, striding on, leaving him and all else. He is here.[47] He stops. You think he is not surprised to see you. He never lost sight of his goal, unlike you. You realise now you got sidetracked often, by many things. But perhaps his goal was easier to keep in mind. It was, after all, only to follow. You had to find something much more difficult to pin down; you still haven't managed to find it, not yet. Find what? And now the game is up.

He approaches you and you have the suspicion that his expression is unbearable in hatred, in triumph. Hide and seek. *Found you.* You can't bring yourself to look at his face to find out. Instead you look at his boots. They are black leather, laced high to the calves. They are shiny, brand new. How could he have walked so far, followed you for so many miles, in those? How many more miles could he go without showing signs of wear?

He comes to you, and stands an arm's length away.

You can't look.

---

47 If we are here, then so is he! There is no escape, not even in the high, rarefied achievement of peace. I've given my dream of a numberless world a name: it's the breathing man. My breathing man.

His body, his manner, is urgent, but he does not speak. He is breathing, of course. You can hear him breathing. Heavy, excited. Or is it just the effort of the climb, the thrill of the chase?

You must risk a look at his face. You have to know if he is planning to hurt you. That is the thought. That he will—batter you, punch you, kick you, bear you to the ground and crush you under his own weight; yes, he will end you. You will be damaged by him. You glance up, just a glance, and see no anger. He is moving his mouth, and his eyes are alight with the need to communicate. The urgency. You hear nothing. He talks without sound, and he is shouting.

381

GOOD, YOU THINK.

You don't want to hear him. You like this insulation from his desire, his emotions. You just want him to go away. You tell him so. *Go away.* You can see the words don't register for him. He frowns at you, mouths his own words some more. What are they? You flap your arms, the confidence in your own voice grows. You can hear it. It's his fault if he can't. *Go away!* you scream. *Go away!*

He stops talking and watches your mouth.

You see desperation building in him.

You shout louder, as if that would make a difference. You know it's no good. But you are determined now. To be louder, stronger. You are not weak.

His face becomes outrage. His eyes darken with it.

You stop shouting.

He lunges for you, fast, and your act folds. Your bravery shrivels. You contract every muscle, you hold yourself still, tight. He is so tall. He is taller, stronger, faster. He will beat you, he will beat you every time. You are not making words any more. You can't find the breath within you to scream, when all you want is to scream and scream, for anybody, *at* anybody. He has all the breath on his side, but even so, even without that basic gift of air, you will resist him.

He is not touching you. He is pointing. Over your shoulder. His finger, adamant, over and over again. *That way. That way.*

You do as he wants.

You face that direction, and you walk. The road. He wants you to follow it, down the hill, and it narrows and becomes little more than a trail thick with pebbles to trip you, but you manage to keep your feet and you make it down to a small natural harbour, set back in the folds of the cliff. The whole time his breath is strong on your neck. He does not touch you. He does not need to. He has you, and he will not let you go.

On the shining shingle, wet from the retreat of the

waves, there is a red boat, small and battered. It looks like a fishing vessel, seaworthy and proven, with a cabin in its middle and rolls of rope upon its sides.

381

YOU LOOK AROUND for help. If there is a fishing boat, isn't there a fisherman? The beach is deserted. His finger stretches out, over your shoulder, to the boat. He means you to get on board, you realise, and you see a version of the future with bright precision—he means to sail you out into waters too deep to survive, and push you overboard. You will drown.

But the deepest part of you asks: why do that when it would be easier to end you here? A strangling. A bashing over the head. You find a sliver of hope in that, and you obey his gesticulation and even help him drag the boat over the shingle, into the water, the two of you working in tandem, applying force to the task. Shoes, socks, trousers, soaked through, until you feel the sea begin to take the boat and you jump in. He pushes hard, up to his waist, and you think maybe he'll trip, or you could push him under, but at that moment he leaps in. Without a glance at you he enters the little cabin and you hear an engine start, the sides and bottom throbbing to its beat, and the smell of diesel mingles with the sharp scent of the sea, and you are lifted by it even as you watch the distance open up between you and the shoreline, and you leave behind everything you know, including the horned road.[48]

Immediately you know you need to return to it.

There is time to plan, to think of a way to escape. This boat is not fast-moving. He leaves you alone, concentrates on steering, and you try to force your mind to make opportunities, consider options.

Attack him, you think, but you know he would win—or, not, it's not that thought of losing. It's about descending to a course of action and then having to live with the consequences, whatever they may be. *If you give way to violence you will deserve what comes next:* that's what you think.

Throw yourself over, you think, but how come the shore already looks so far away? You thought everything was happening slowly, not in this double time, and now you can't be sure you can swim.

Can you swim?

---

48 I breathe in a great world. I know this because I have studied other times, other places, and there is not one single human being who would not have preferred this version. All major problems solved, peace achieved: what use the quest? But there must be a quest, there must be, because beyond the role of the hero, the achievement of greatness, there is also the small voice within which says: *What am I here for?* And if that is not a valid question by Dr Magnaman's standards then I can't keep faith with him any longer.

YOU WERE ONCE taken to the seaside by Cecile and her father.[49] She had one of those professional working fathers who fancied himself a sailor, and had bought a trailer and a rowboat as an antidote to the commuting life to Telezon every day. A peaked cap completed his transformation. Most weekends for a year were taken up with the trip to the boat for Cecile, her time being fed to his fantasy: *get in, here we go, here we go*. The drive to a little seaside bay, winding through its bright houses, then splatting about with oars and the preparation of the fishing lines along with the other weekend sailors. Cecile said: *do you want to come?* and made a face. You said yes. Your mother would never have taken you and you wanted to find out what having a father was like, even one that made you do boring activities.

When it came to a question of loyalty, you sided with Cecile, of course, and the two of you laughed at her father. He never realised. He thought his enthusiasm

---

49 I've never actually been out on the water, for all my love of seafaring. Ahoy. They say the best way to see the Unity Spire is from the lake surrounding it. Water is cold and fresh and clean on the skin. Water, fire, air, life. Today I'm wearing a warm woollen garment made from well-cared-for sheep, and it is just a little itchy. It's made that way, deliberately. Just a little itchiness. Maybe a body should never be without it.

was infectious, not ridiculous. His fingers constantly found their way to the peak of his cap. He gave you an oar each and told you to try rowing. It was tough work, you thought you were barely moving, but when you looked behind you the sea had done what you could not, and moved you far, far out from the shore. The laughter left you.

The father smiled kindly, and took the oars from you both. He rowed you back, his muscles working hard, and you sat in misery. Later, your mother asked you how it was, and you said you didn't like sailing, and she nodded as if she had expected as much. You wished you'd been a person that did like it, just to spite her.

The next weekend Cecile was made to go again, and she asked if you wanted to come along. You pretended to think about it and then said no. You let her down.

She had to go. She had no choice. The demand of this time spent together, the sickness of the rocking rowboat, continued for the rest of that year, and then the weather grew cold, and the father's passion waned.

381

THIS BOAT IS bigger, this sea is rougher. The breathing man is not your saviour, or your father, or any type of man you've known in your limited experience, and the very nature of his impassive steering over choppy waters is what makes you think he is not planning to return to land, ever. You wish you had appreciated the land before you were taken from it. You wished you had hugged your body to it, even to the stones that tripped you.

Up ahead you see the horizon.

You stare hard, over the side of the boat, directing your eyes forward. At length the horizon turns from a far line to a white strip with rising hills of green above, and then nuances of colour arrive: speckles, clusters of shapes, brown dots that become houses on the shore. This feels very familiar to you, but it can't be: you've never left your own land before—how can this new land, over water, be in your mind already? But no, no, soon it begins to coalesce into difference. Only the general nature of the seaside town is familiar, from this distance. Just like that one time you went fishing with Cecile's father. The line of houses and the masts in the harbour. Are some things the same the world over?

The breathing man is steering the boat to the town.

You try to think of how to use this. How close do you need to get before you'll jump, or scream, or lock desperate eyes on someone who might help? Even if you must bide your time on arrival, you feel sure you could find aid there, lose him among the colourful facades and touristy shops.

But you realise the boat is not aiming directly for the town. He is not steering for it, and over the minutes that pass you see how you are being taken out in a curve following the headland to a small beach just like the one you left behind. The cliffs are sheer and grey, white birds nesting, flying on and off jutting rocks. And on the beach, one eye-catching splash of colour: a pink pavilion with a pointed silk roof and billowing sides, caught in the wind that runs along the sand so freely.

381

HOW CAN THAT *be here?* you think.

You once dreamed of a place like this. You asked your mother for a tent just like it, and she put up sheets in the garden, over the washing line, held in place with pegs. It stirred you in a way you could not explain, did not want to examine. You sat in it for hours, until it had to be taken down when bad weather threatened. Could it have been a premonition? Surely you don't believe in that. That road only runs in one direction—from the past to the future, no stopping, only these mournful glances behind you—and you are sick of it, sick of looking over your shoulder and seeing nothing there that can make any difference. Fuck the past.

The boat approaches the shore, the waves building, grabbing at the bow, and the breathing man cuts the engine, emerges from the cabin without a glance in your direction and throws down an anchor. Yards from the beach, he jumps down into the water and holds out his arms to you.

You won't touch him.

You won't put him in the position where he feels it is acceptable to touch you.

You get up and jump over the other side of the boat, nearly fall flat into the waves, but you flail, steady yourself, and start striding to the beach. You hurry. You beat him to the pavilion, pushing aside the gleaming pink curtain at the entryway to find just enough room to stand inside. Where will he go? Surely he can't mean to come in here too, but yes, here he is, he is pushing his way in through the curtain, having to stoop to fit under the billowing roof and somehow he manages to get entirely inside without touching you once. You do not collide, but you are face to face, you cannot bear to look, you must look. He breathes on you. His breath is pressure. You put your hands up to your mouth, your elbows out, sharp points. You close your eyes, cannot bear it, open your eyes again.

Then you hear drumming.

Drumming across the sand.

The walls of the tent ripple.

The drumming gets louder.

The walls billow.

It is the drumming of feet.

381

PEOPLE ARE COMING for you. What have you done? You must deserve it: his eyes tell you so. You must deserve this, and you should know why, and it goes to the heart of you. You are a terrible quester. You were seen. Whatever it was you did or didn't do, it was seen by the breathing man and by the creators of these footfalls. They are disturbing the sand, making the patterns of a mob. When they arrive the thin silk walls will be no protection. They are nearly upon you.

I'm sorry! you cry. They couldn't possibly hear you; you can hardly hear yourself over the racket they create. The breathing man frowns at you. Another mistake on your part.

And then

the drumming stops

so abrupt

that the silence left behind is LOUD

everything is loud

your own breathing is loud

your own breathing and the

breathing of the breathing man

Slow, relentless, he breathes like a machine, like a given right, and your own breath feels stolen, feels like a punishment.

I'm sorry, you whisper.

Are you sorry?

Sorry for speaking, doing, *daring* to do. Sorry for being one thing and not another. Sorry for all the things that have been before, for what you knew about those things and what you never knew. Sorry to take up space. Sorry for your characteristics and the arrangement of your face, and it is enough, you see it in his eyes, hear it in the loudest silence of your life. He realises you are sorry, and you are nothing because of it. Worse than a person.

He steps back, just enough for you to squeeze past him without touching. You manage it, and you are so grateful for his mercy. You smell his perfect breath, once, on your forehead, and then you push through the silk and face whatever waits outside.

There is nothing there.

The beach is empty, and the boat sits lonely in the sea. The sea is very smooth, waveless. Where have the waves gone?

You turn, and put your fingers to the opening of the tent. You dare to twitch them apart. You find the breathing man has gone.

You realise this is not any kind of end.

This is where the game begins again.

381

But still, this gives you breathing space. You feel lighter. Calmer. You consider your options.

Do you get back in the waiting boat and try to sail back to pick up the horned road where you left off?

You do not.

Do you attempt to sail, knowing you are not a good sailor, to a new and better place?

You do not.

Do you sit down and wait for the breathing man to come again? You can feel the relief of his distance; he is far away, you're certain of it. You have no idea how he travelled so quickly. But he will come back, you know that too. Perhaps he won't. But you know he will. So, will you wait for him, accept that this cycle in which you find yourself is part of your uselessness?

You do not.

You walk along the beach.

You move inland to a shallow cove until you find a dune leading to an opening through the grasses that line the hills behind it. This is hard walking on your stiff legs, and your muscles tire quickly. You need food, and rest. You need good human faces to smile at you.

The seaside town.

It couldn't be far away. You glance around, and wish so hard for the road—delineated, described and designed by those who have come before—to place your feet upon. You'd like to think you have a decent sense of direction, and surely you only need to follow the coast, right? You came from the sea, but in that direction, right? You can do this. You can find that town, and make the locals love you, and they will take you in and cherish you and feed you and give you a bed to sleep in so you don't have to go into another tent ever again. You are aware that this is, on some level, a piece of ridiculousness. But haven't you been through enough? Don't you deserve to cherish your optimistic idiocy for once? You are in need of kind human company, maybe even love. The desire for it is as strong as hunger, as pervasive as the need for sleep.

You guess at the direction, you hope for the best, you dream of the ultimate, and you walk.[50]

---

50 The trick is not in following the road, but in finding the road in the first place – yes, the *question*, the question is all-important! We all travel to find the question, not the answer! Faith in the Magnaman method is restored. Reading of the past is as close as we will ever get to time travel. There are moments where the words dissolve and there is no barrier between the thoughts and feelings on the page and in your life. I understand. I claim the incomprehensible as my own experience, for what part of any of it – real or imagined – could anyone say makes sense?

THE SEASIDE TOWN is busy. The pubs are loud, the smell of food is hot and greasy and as thick on the streets as litter. People everywhere, dressed for better weather, as if they can will away the clouds. There are signs for boat rides, horse rides, wild rides, casinos. Every corner is a photo opportunity, even when there is nothing to see.

You could forget yourself here. Be of no compunction, no quest, and no time at all.

You choose a pub at random—the Jolly Anchor—and enter, and find yourself in familiar territory. It is similar to the bar in Telezon. The barman even looks the same (what was his name? you can't remember his name, but it was just last week, wasn't it, and he was your only friend—his name was Sam, you can't believe you nearly forgot that), and he nods as if he knows you. It freaks you out. You leave.

The idea of a hotel appeals.

A bed and breakfast.

What about the cost?

You'll haggle.

Your mother told you about a time she went away for a weekend with your father—a figure long shrouded in too much exotic mystery to ever feel even slightly real to you—and ate an enormous breakfast, packed with protein. That's how she described it. You feel like you need to be packed with protein right now. It sounds soothing.

The Forever stands on a back street behind the sea wall, tall and thin, like one yellowed tooth in the bottom row of a characterful old mouth. You like the net curtains and the dusty porch with etched glass. You're a little afraid of the woman behind the mahogany reception desk. She looks forbidding, with severe glasses and hairstyle, but she looks you over and nods.

'On the house for questers,' she says. You want to ask: How can you get questers when you're not on the horned road? But you're too tired to care. She assigns you a small room at the top of the hotel looking out over the sea, back towards where you came from.

You sink down on the bed, the smell of cigarettes impregnated into the meadow print coverlet, and sleep the sleep of the dead. The stolen. The returned.

381

YOU WAKE FEELING like an old person in a young body. You look in the mirror over the little sink and wish for your experiences so far to show on your face. The feeling of being in the pavilion: you can still conjure it. It's only just under the surface. But when you do, it's not there in the mirror at all.

Bed and breakfast.

You head downstairs for protein. It's a mission, better than any stupid quest you've been attempting to complete up until this point. Clear, simple. Protein. And there is lots of it on the plate that comes your way. Meat. Delicious. You push away the thought of the cha, and tuck into strips of meat, rolls of meat, discs of meat. It doesn't taste like cha, does it? You're not sure, and you're too hungry to let it stop you. You have feelings about eating cha, but as long as you don't look too closely at the feelings they'll probably go away.

Your table is in the centre of the room, small and round, with one chair. Couples and families are arranged around you, all faces seeming to point to you. You wonder if you are here as an attraction. There is only one other single diner, and she is seated not far from you, at a rectangular table near a fireplace which must be a leftover from when this high-ceilinged room was something else.

'Healthy appetite,' she calls to you. She is eating toast. Then she says, 'They can solve basic puzzles, you know.'

Cha?

They can do more than that. They can manage mountain chalets and hot tubs. You don't say this, and the woman continues, 'Pigs. I supply hotels like the Forever with their pig products. Only the best.'

She is dressed in layers of grey wool, each piece overlapping the other to create an outfit that resembles protection; you wish you had style like it. 'The best hotels or the best pigs?' you say, emboldened by protein, and she laughs at your joke.

'Both,' she says, and you fall in love. It's instant and painless and it's exactly what you needed.[51] You've slept, your stomach is full, and the woman tells you to move your chair to her table, so you can talk.

381

NOT IN LOVE so much, you decide, quite early on into your conversation, but in love with the immediate sense of passion she projects, which is surprising considering she's just sitting there eating toast. But she really is passionate, and her focus is pigs. You wish you felt so strongly about your quest, or about any aspect of your life. You are envious with every part of you, even the traumatised, guilty, frozen part deep inside that you're

---

51 'Love at First Sight' is one of the key concepts that dominates and perpetuates itself throughout this age, love being one of those ideal states of pleasure/pain in which everyone was meant to be, in some way. One could be in it, or out of it. 381 is love. The interiority of the consciousness, trapped in the wanting, needing body, meant that the feelings of the other party/parties involved were considered relevant, but essentially unknowable. See: *Optimal Suffering – States of Ecstasy and Swiping Right* by the RNA (DDD45922294).

Will I fall in love myself, one day? I don't have forever.

busy pretending doesn't exist. Perhaps with that part more than any other. How can you get to feel that way? Do you need to accomplish something first?

'The name's Fortune,' she says, and sticks out her hand, and when you take it, you feel the roughness of hard work, pig work. It must be physically as well as emotionally demanding.

This new emotion of love quickly takes charge of you, and you're only five minutes into your conversation when you tell her that you've always been interested in pig rearing. She expresses gratified surprise, and you end up agreeing that you are so alike, you and Fortune, and you abandon any thought of regaining the horned road and decide to go and work alongside her at her farm instead.

The older woman who had been so impressed at check-in is not so awed at check-out. She frowns as Fortune talks on about the room you can have at the farm, and the work you'll be doing; *You're meant to be on a quest*, her eyes seem to say, but she does not speak it aloud. It would be difficult for her to interrupt Fortune's excited speech without appearing rude, anyway.

Fortune says things about how pigs work and what pigs like, and what they need on a daily basis, which is food and water and, yes, love. It sounds like she's given this speech before, and you wonder if this is the first time she's tempted somebody into her profession. Perhaps there's powerful magic in the morning bacon. The older woman is winking at you. Is this a warning? Too late now: you've thrown over one destiny for another. You follow Fortune to her car, climb in, and let her drive you to her farm, which is not very far away at all.

381

CHA.

'They're not pigs. They're cha,' you say.

She laughs at you. 'Good one,' she says.

The cha stand in loose formation, close to a rusted, mud-caked trough close to a fence. Fortune has one foot on the sturdy gate that keeps them in. The mud has wiped off on her soft grey ensemble, but she doesn't seem to care. What an inspiring person she is. You still sort of love her, even if she's mocking you, or doesn't understand you, or something.

You check again.

Yes, these are cha. Fluffy round bodies, little triangular ears. You should know. They let you use their hot tub.

You hate to disagree with someone so impressive, but you've just realised you're determined to be honest at the start of this new relationship. 'Seriously, aren't they cha?' you say. Perhaps this is a test. You try to sound more certain of yourself. 'Yes, cha.'

'I've been in the pig industry for twenty years,' she says, her eyes wide, as if she can't believe what you're saying. It's a joke to her. A bad joke. 'Do I cha farm? No. I pig farm. What even is a cha? Never heard of it.'

'You don't know what a cha is?'

'I know what pigs are. I know all about what pigs do. I know what pigs say. They say *oink*.' She turns to the nearest cha, who has been listening to this exchange with great interest. 'What do pigs say?' she asks it.

'Oink,' it says, obligingly.

'Everyone,' Fortune says, raising her voice to the whole herd of cha. 'What do you say?'

There's a moment where you think they'll do something. You're not sure what. Laugh at her, or ignore her, or tell her the truth. Don't they know how important the truth is? *I know cha*, you want to say. *I worked in a bar. I let go of the hand of a girl. I listened to stampeding hordes in a silk pavilion, and I sailed over a sea. Be honest. Particularly now, at the start of this wonderful new life.*

'Oink,' say all the cha, at once, and you doubt everything, all over again. It is awful. The dream is broken. You're not in faux love, or any sort of love, after all.[52]

---

52 If I do fall in love, I hope it lasts longer than it does for Fairly. Calculations of variance of length of love suggests 'love' (see the 478,973,003 metatags currently listed under Romantic Love) could last for any period of time, from seconds to centuries – beyond life, into death, even before streaming synthesis was achieved. Another great big adventure for the brave to enjoy.

YOU'RE NOT SURE what the cha are getting out of this.

Every day you feed them and stroke them and chat to them, and when Fortune is not around you ask them, quietly, 'What's in it for you?' They never answer with anything other than an oink. They are committed, you give them that. But the day will come—the day will come when they are taken away to become bacon and sausages. That can't possibly be what they want. Maybe they're not aware of their fate. You want to tell them, but you can't start that conversation, not when they caper around so happily.

You wonder if your advance knowledge of the end process would upset you so much if you were certain these were pigs, real pigs, properly destined for sanctioned, agreeable slaughter.

You start to think a lot about that moment when you found the corpses of the cha from the mountain chalet. That massacre. The butchery.

You want to speak to your mother.

Fortune has a chime. You've seen it in the main house, on a small table in the hall. Everything in her house is as chic and coordinated as she is, even the items in the spare room, in which you stay without ever leaving a trace of yourself. You make the beautiful slim bed as soon as you get up every day, and you haven't dared to unpack your backpack.

You ask her if you can chime, one evening, after dinner, and she says, *Yes, of course, whenever you like!* So you pick up the receiver, tentatively, and there is the voice of home: your mother. You thought you might cry, or beg for her to come and take you home, but the sound of her is enough to prove that you are not the daughter she knew any more, even though she recognises your sound straight away. You couldn't possibly explain what you're going through, so you say you are fine, just tired, and maybe you've lost your way, and she says:

Sometimes we lose our way to find it again.[53]

Does that help? It does help.

And yes, you definitely have changed, for sure. You feel stronger, cooler. Damaged and glued back together with a super substance. You feel like an adult.

381

EVERYONE IS STILL clinging to their roles, and you are a pig farmer now. You try to think and act like a pig farmer.

It turns out it's easier, as a pig farmer, to watch things move towards an inexorable conclusion without worrying about it too much. You manage to feel quite

---

53 There's a possible idea for further study, here: the sayings of Fairly's mother cross-catalogued and compared with identified idioms of the time. Or maybe organic life is too fucking short.

distant from the future butchery, right up until the day it comes around.

A truck arrives from the slaughterhouse, and you begin to help in the process of loading the pig-pretending cha on board. Surely they know what's happening. You expect rebellion. You expect them to suddenly say, in human voices: *Say what?* What would they say? You can only think of things you might say, which is not the same thing at all.

You can also think of things your mother might say, in that calm tone of voice she employs at the chime. You realise you know everything she might say for any circumstance, after years of listening to her at work. It triggers something in you. A desire to not let this go to a story you tell later, or an epithet.

You lean close to a cha at the back of the truck as you help to seal up the doors, and tell it, 'It's now or never.'

It fixes you with an even stare and says, slowly, deliberately, drawing out the syllable, 'Oink.'

So you seal the truck and Fortune comes to your other and side-hugs you as you both wave the cha goodbye. She sheds a tear. 'It's emotional,' she says. How wonderful it is, to be both the mother and the murderer of so many.

A new truck pulls up.

You help to open the door, and inside, blinking away at the admittance of light, are very small cha. Babies, you guess. They are adorable.

'Here we go again,' said Fortune, with a sigh, and you start the business of unloading.

At that point you begin to wonder if there really is any such things as pigs, or if that's a lie you've been told. What if all meat is cha? Has always been cha? What are cha, anyway? Are they really all the same thing, from the hot tub to the fairy tale to the spit in the cave? To this?[54]

381

SO WHAT, THOUGH? you think, that night, in the slim borrowed bed. *So what?* It appears to be their choice to impersonate, to play the role. They stand and sit where they are told, they sleep when the sun goes down and say oink in the sunshine.

You ask Fortune if she thinks pigs are intelligent.

'They can solve basic puzzles,' she says. 'Watch.'

She goes to the house and returns with a board game.

---

54 Cha (cha cha cha?) move from folklore to hard currency to saviours to food sources to dissemblers – to where? I can see the beginning of the deepening of a central mystery to a possible conspiracy theory (CON3494343811), a key concept of the Age of Riches often attributed to a growing sense of dissatisfaction/ disbelief in world events due to the stretching of the fabric of reality by the growth of the virtual (Reality dissonance: WTF45439544) .

The cha, delighted, sit around it in the pen and play a few games, dividing into teams with lots of organisational oinking.

You say that looks pretty complex to you, and wonder aloud about free will. Fortune says, 'What's that?'

It turns out Fortune is not as cool as she looks. In fact, you can begin to see that she's not that great, really. She cares, absolutely, but maybe caring isn't enough. Not when it comes from a place of ignorance. Caring can be worse than not giving a shit, when you're deluded.

Unless you're the deluded one, in which case: caring is all there is.

In the aftermath of that revelation you start having nightmares. You don't remember what happens in them. You only know that you wake up sweating and you feel profoundly saddened by yourself. You feel shame.

If you could make all the decisions here, you would free all the cha in the land. But if you could make decisions for other people, you have the feeling a world of horror would be unleashed. You're not that good at making decisions. You wish somebody brilliant would make the decisions instead, and always get it right.

'Are you all right?' Fortune asks you, over a lunch of light salad, and you nod, but you can see she's aware the magic has gone out of your relationship.

It can't be denied any longer. You have to make

decisions for yourself. Nobody else can be trusted, and it means everything will always be a mess, but there it is. You understand this upon waking on the morning that Fortune is returning to town. You will leave while she is away. You make that decision, and the shame lifts. You won't raise these cha to die. It's not rebellion, but it's the best you can do.[55]

381

YOU WAVE FORTUNE goodbye, and then return to the borrowed room, smooth down the duvet on the slim bed once more, and collect your backpack.

You will leave.

But you must see the cha before you go.

In their warm dark, strong smell, shit-squishy shed, they stand on hay and regard you. Nobody oinks. Nobody dares.

You whisper, 'Tell me.'

They raise their eyebrows. You reach over the metal bar, hesitate. Then you stroke the hard, tiny triangle ears of the nearest cha.

---

55 Are these the kinds of decisions people from the Age of Riches had to make all the time? To abandon what's best for the world and concentrate only on what makes for a better person, as if the two are divisible?

Are the two divisible?

'Tell me.'

Is it your imagination, or do its eyes dart to your left?

There it is again.

That subtle glance to the left.

Then it lowers its head and steps back.

You move, slowly, trance-like, over there. This part of the shed is a pile of forgotten objects, heaped high, dusty tarpaulin strapped across mechanical junk. You find the tight ropes that hold the tarp and, with some effort, manage to loosen them. The tarp slips, and you pull it back. You see diggers and planters and so many objects that you can't identify, all of them rusting together peacefully, and you also see—

A chain device.

It's just the same as the one that you pressed when you first started this adventure, and the same again as the one that stood on the cliff edge, before the breathing man arrived. You had thought him far away but time has passed and things have changed and he could be here, could be just outside. You feel the possibility of it and your throat is so tight you can't swallow. You look around the shed, out into the sunshine. He's not there. There is nobody here. Only the cha, who are attentive, wary, all turned to you, all watching. Their faces seem to ask you a question:

Will you press the button?

You don't know.

You thought you'd left the quest behind. The quest involves pressing the buttons. You imagined you'd changed, you had rejected being a quester. You wanted to be a farmer, there, for a brief moment. That time has passed. So why not be a quester again? Yes, back to the quest. Not for your mother or your town or for the sake of propriety. For the sake of finding out how the quest ends.

381

So YOU PRESS the button, and at first it seemed as though nothing had changed. The cha pretending to be pigs stopped staring and milled about, looking less intelligent by the moment. The chain device was the same—or was it? For the more she looked at it the smaller it seemed to get, and when she blinked to clear her confused eyes it disappeared altogether, and that was that. No sign it had ever existed. Only a space around the junk of the barn, and the will to walk came to her, came to her strongly.

Backpack shouldered, she headed out, determined to leave the farm far behind—to find more chain devices, to move on again and again. It had an addictive quality, this business of bringing things to an end.

As she walked, Fairly's mind kept returning to the way the device had disappeared. It was concerning to think they could come and go as they wanted, and so it was not a case of finding them, but somehow triggering them. Which made the act of geographically seeking them out seem... pointless.

Even so, she followed the road.

It wasn't the horned road. But it stretched before her, took her miles, with meadows on either side in pleasant weather. Then the meadows bulged and tangled, and the road petered out into a path, then little more than a trail. Trees sprang up and began to crowd out the sunlight. The ground became littered with leaf mulch, peppered with tiny fungi, delicate and transparent. How damp it was. Swampy. Fairly realised it was autumn. Hadn't it been spring when she'd first set out on this adventure? Soon it would be winter, and the world would grow weary. She was an idiot for leaving that warm borrowed bed behind, perhaps, but the desire to go on, to solve, was still strong. It hadn't faded in the course of a single afternoon, which was a relief. Maybe she did have some backbone after all.

So she carried on walking until there was no trail left to follow, and any direction was as good as another. Then she stopped and looked around, and tried to discern the swamp as a place of its own order rather than the mess it looked like.

381

IT DID POSSESS order, but it was skyward, not at her eyeline; Fairly looked up and around in wonder at the way the drab leaves collected in balls, grew in patterns, never touching but allowing threads of weak sunlight to penetrate in places. The old, gnarled trees were magnificent—why hadn't she seen it before? She walked on, her feet sinking into mud, her eyes raised, watching the movement of the branches in the wind. She was seeing the great beauty of a fleeting time.

Men.

There were men crouching in the treetops.

They could have been mistaken for knobbled growths on the branches, lying long and flat, pressed into position. But once she had seen them, she was certain. Men. She passed underneath them, taking each step carefully, not daring to take her eyes from them. They had wild, tufted hair and long brown cloaks, and their fingers were curled around the bark. If they were watching her, they did not show it. Their faces were hidden under mud, dirt, that mad outcropping hair.

Wild men?

'I see you,' she said.

Let them make of her what they would.

They straightened, stood tall on the trees. She was surrounded by them. A large number. One of them, directly ahead of her, jumped down lightly. She would never have risked leaping such a distance herself, but it came easily to him, and this show of immediate, powerful athleticism set her nerves on edge. She felt the presence of him in some way she could not describe, had not come across before.

He fixed her with a solemn stare and threw back his brown cloak. Underneath he wore grey trousers, a white shirt. They looked pressed, cared for. He was not a wild man at all. He made a small gesture with one hand, the pinching together of thumb and forefinger, and the other men descended, falling to their feet around her, just as she had pictured the leaves falling, and she understood that the season had changed while she had been standing there. There was a long winter ahead.

But the first to fall from the tree, the one directly before her, was the lightest and the best, she thought. And with that realisation she fell in love all over again.

381

THEY TOOK HER back to their home.

Fairly supposed these sudden devotions she had started to develop—Fortune the pig farmer, now the First to Fall—were an example of how she ran in small circles, covering much ground but no distance. Her heart worked fast, her body ached. And the sudden love she felt was not mental. She was only beginning to understand that it really had little to do with her brain. It was all physical. She wanted the First to Fall to be inside her. There was an actual space he could fill. He, and his brothers: the disgraced and exiled family of the Royal House of Warfarin.[56]

They told her all about themselves around the cooking pot in the communal space on stilts in their aerial home; a series of walkways and cabins above the sucking swamp, closed in by a great stockade of cut wood. They had the easy camaraderie and well-worn tensions of a large family, but also the instant watchfulness of those who had been hunted, which made conversation difficult. Every time Fairly began to enjoy the banter, they broke off to stare at the edges of the light. Attuned, sharp.

The First to Fall, the one she loved, tilted his head at her and said, 'Where are you from?'

'Overseas,' she said, which brought painful memories, and to her twisted face he nodded. He said, 'You look like one who's met the breathing man.'

'I...'

---

56 Warfarin (anticoagulant) triggers many associations, none of which relate to Royal Houses that have been documented. Could there be a connection between drug companies and perceived royalty? Or possibly this is a corruption of the document or a play on words. Basically, I don't know. I don't know, I don't know. I'm lost in history. Help me.

'He can't reach us here.'

Yes, she knew him, and she was amazed that they knew him too, and guarded against him. How did they keep him out? Did this intense watchfulness work? The First to Fall told her, then, of the breathing man's plot to bring down the Warfarin line, to make them bleed, and how their unrelenting quest to destroy him had ended up turning their own people against them.

'They did not understand,' said the First to Fall, and his brothers nodded. She counted at least thirty of them. 'What did he do to you?'

She wanted to tell him, but she could not speak of the breathing man.

The First to Fall squeezed her hand in sympathy, and he talked instead while the food cooked in the pot and the night grew long.

381

THE FIRST TO FALL said:

We thought we'd come here, to the swamp, to wallow in our shame, to sit around and be the lowest of the low, but it turns out that being born to rule is difficult to forget, and so is the desire for dry feet, so we built this raised place and began to rule ourselves. For a while we thought we had survived the worst, but it turns out the worst is only ever up ahead in our minds and never in the present or past. It's a quality, not an absolute. Do you know what I mean? Nobody knows that better than the breathing man. He found us and stood underneath us, all day, all night. We threatened him and we tried to make him leave, but we aren't warriors! He could see straight through our promises to hurt him. He became cockier. More confident. He began to come into the communal area, and stand in the corner, in the dark. We couldn't sleep.

We built the stockade.

It's not a good stockade, because we aren't carpenters either, but we are learning. We learn more every day, and we find food, and we do upkeep on the stockade, and all's well. Except that there is always a hole somewhere, do you know what I mean? There is always a part of the stockade that is failing, a part not as tight, and if the breathing man finds it, he can look at us, work out our weaknesses. Maybe find a way to squeeze through.

It's a lot of hard work to live this way.

We all miss the days of ease and splendour, with servants and copious food that didn't taste of mud and our own sweat. But we have learned to get by with what we have. Would you like to learn that trick?

Smoky space, twilight, the touch of his hand. Hot food. Cool water. Up high in the strong trees, safe there, high above threats, secure in the stockade. Fairly sighed. She did not think their breathing man was quite the same as her breathing man. But it was close enough, and the stockade might just deter him too.

If love wasn't the pooling of defences, she didn't know what it was.

381

His presence was a balm to her.

He and his brothers were a wonderfully oiled machine of living. They collaborated and cooperated. They moved as one when they hunted, and they broke apart to patrol the stockade with a strength of purpose that gave her deep, squirming feelings. They kept a routine that passed effortlessly to her, and she became a piece of their lives so quickly that she could almost forget the life she'd had before.

The First to Fall was obviously the centre of her new existence, but she never said that out loud to his brothers. She decided she would never speak of her preference.

At night, on the communal platform, Fairly began to tell her own stories. She even managed to speak a little of her breathing man. But every time she spoke of him, he changed. She couldn't capture how she had felt in his presence, or why she had felt compelled to act in the way she had. Why had she let him chase her down to the shore, or stand in the pavilion? It all seemed less like any sort of reality she could relate to. The stories moved into fantasies in which she acted differently, thought differently, and that was fine too. The Warfarin brothers cheered the stories as she tweaked them, made them more exciting and less inexplicable, and they flowed more and more easily from her mouth.

The price of all this relaxation and removal from herself seemed cheap at first.

She took it upon herself to care for the stockade. She found a patch that the others often overlooked, and she attended it daily. It was just outside the public convenience hut, where the smell tended to dominate, but she didn't mind. She liked having a place to go, a task to do. And the wood seemed strong in that location, tough. Impenetrable.

But the more she looked after it, the more she began to notice the tiny cracks in the grain. The wood was wearing down. It might, one day, split.

After a while the watchfulness of the Warfarins began to seep into her. Everything might be fine right now, but how long would now last? She was ever more vigilant.

And then, one day, she found a hole.

381

OF COURSE.

Of course there was a hole.

It had been inevitable.

Fairly stuck her finger through it.

On the other side of the hole, the air felt different. Colder.

She steeled herself, pulled out her finger, and put her eye to it. She had thoughts in her head of what she might see. A man. There was no need to say what man. His head. His eye, level with hers. There was nothing. Well, there was the swamp. She heard rustling leaves and she felt that both something and nothing was out there. She didn't know what she wanted or hated more.

There was no wind.

The sound of leaves rustling, and no wind.

A breath.

The breathing man: she could hear him. She couldn't see him. Was she certain? It could be her imagination. She remembered a time, back at the beginning of the quest, when he had been on the other side of a wall, and his breathing was her companion when she woke.

She did not speak. Neither did he. If he was there. If he was there.

'A hole,' said a voice, behind her, and she pulled back and nodded to one of the brothers. His familiar face should have soothed her. She had no idea which brother it was—not the First to Fall, anyway. But she was not sure even the First to Fall could have calmed her at that moment.

'A hole,' he said again, louder, and then he called it out,

over and over. 'A hole, a hole!' The others came running—nobody bothered about the smell when something so important was happening—and they brought supplies ready for the job of fixing it, with nails and wood and glue they'd made from some old bones and soon, with industrious concentration, the hole was taken care of.

'It's all right,' said the brothers, to each other, to her. Their relief was catching; it spread to Fairly, and it seemed the day was saved.

They all retired to the communal area. They asked her for a story, and when she started to tell them the story of finding the hole they shushed her, and said, 'Not that, a real story.' She made something up, and they were all a lot happier.

381

AFTER THAT THERE was a smattering of holes most days. The discovery of each one caused consternation, and offered a fresh glimpse of the empty and teeming swamp outside.

Then, just as it seemed the whole thing might tip into a plethora of holes that would defeat them, the holes stopped appearing.

By this point Fairly had become the lover of the First to Fall. It had been inevitable, she thought, in retrospect, although she had agonised over the decision. But if not him, who? When? And then, when the other brothers started to look sad, she loved them too, in turn, without any shame or friction. They never asked for the company of her body, but she liked the gentle gratitude she found in their touch. She did not always enjoy the sex. But it obliterated past, future, consequence. Her body felt used for this purpose, thoroughly, and it was good and true.

The First to Fall remained her real love; she felt certain he knew it. They never spoke of it.

They never spoke of anything important, she realised, and came to understand that was, along with the stockade, a major element of their defensive capability.

It was a wonderful time.

But still—the stockade.

The stockade now had no holes.

She couldn't explain it, but she knew what she had to do to relieve the tension it brought her, like a deep itch, or a blister that must be burst.

She made a hole of her own.

She returned to the spot of the first hole, ignoring the smell, and took a sharp rock to a spot beside the repair. The relief as the rock scraped through the wood was enormous. Tears sprang to her eyes. It was better than sex. She picked the splinters from the wound and put her watering gaze to the hole. Yes, the outside was there. The swamp, the trees, the murk.

The sound of breathing.

She moved away.

Later that day the cry of 'Hole!' went up. It had been discovered. Everyone came together and fixed it, and she was happy to have given them a purpose once more. It was addictive, to be so central to everyone's wellbeing, in the here and now. She wanted to live there forever.[57]

381

MAKING HOLES IN the stockade became a pattern, then a mission. Then a quest. Dare she admit it to herself? Yes, it was her new quest: an action she undertook relentlessly, with determination, without knowing what the end point might be.

Then the end point came.

She was caught in the act of making a hole.

It was the First to Fall who found her. She had just drilled through with her sharp stone, was experiencing the high, giddy relief it gave her, when her hand was grabbed and pulled, and she spun around to find herself looking at the agonised face of her love. She burst into tears.

'Oh, no,' he said. 'No.'

There was a process for her crime, which made her

---

57 Stockades and holes: there have been hints of the ideals of the walled village/separate life throughout, although how this relates to

suspect somebody had done it before. Was she really the first woman to live here? It was yet another discussion nobody would have, but they were happy to inform her all about the trial and how that would work, and she tried to listen, but she had got out of the habit. Or perhaps she'd never been good at it. She couldn't remember.

On the day of the trial, she stood in the centre of their circle. They took turns pointing at her and declaring her guilty. It didn't feel like much of a trial; it was over in minutes. And at the moment of the delivery of the verdict—banishment, to be implemented immediately— Fairly felt her stomach drop, her skin freeze: what had she thrown away? It was awful on the other side of the stockade, without protection, without the bodies of the Warfarin brothers in her and with her.

'I won't do it again,' she said, but she knew that was a lie, and they all frowned at her for speaking. But she couldn't help it; she couldn't be alone again. She turned to the First to Fall, and said, 'Come with me, please, I love you, I can't be without you.'

'Yes,' he said. 'I will.'

Everyone looked incredibly surprised. She imagined that hadn't happened last time around. *He must really love me*, she thought, which made her feel both amazed and alarmed, and unsure as to whether she did really love him. No, she must—she must, or she wouldn't have asked.

381

HE MADE A backpack to match hers, and they stepped out into the swamp.

The sense of the breathing man was strong.

He was everywhere nearby and not even close.

'Let's walk,' she said, and she set off, and it was a miracle how he came with her, obedient, determined, and somehow much smaller than he'd seemed before.

Freed from the family, Fairly dared to ask him to talk about himself, and it seemed the more he did, the more there was to uncover. He was making it up as he went along, she decided, and she liked him more for being prepared to make that effort on her behalf.

Being raised as royalty

—he said, coughed then continued—

was a wonderful experience, particularly since I had survivalist parents who came from a long line of monarchs who had been deposed and reinstated on a regular basis, so they taught me all I would need to know to take care of myself. And it was not fitting for me to practise this knowledge, so I'd watch keen underlings do it, which is the next best thing, do you know what I mean?

She took his hand as they walked.

I was the firstborn, and I helped to train all my brothers in the art of survival too, and we were such a good team we started our own religion called Warfarinism. And when my parents died in a freak stockpiling accident, my brothers and I decided to make Warfarinism the main religion of our country, which went well, we thought. People need leadership, do you know—?

She nodded. She did know what he meant.

He was full of stories about the first stockades they built, and how to chop wood effectively. Fences made of the magic of your own hands. Fence love. All about barriers, and why they need to be kept strong.

The world respects strength, he said.

She couldn't help but notice how he glanced around the swamp. She knew who he was looking for. But she didn't even want to speak of it. How difficult relationships were, with the things that she would and wouldn't say, could and couldn't love. They walked until nightfall, and then she set up her tent and they crawled into the tiny space.

381

HE WANTED THE comfort of her body, and she wanted the comfort of his. *Forget brains and stories*, she said to herself, and surrendered herself to his long fingers, soft mouth, the rough skin of his cheeks and the sigh he poured forth that was lean and hungry for her. She was a meal to him. She was eaten.

The next morning, they did the same again as a talisman against the day ahead, and afterwards she asked him, 'Where are we going?'

'I don't know,' he said.

She felt delicate from his devourment. She let him lead the way, and saw how he picked certain routes, veered to the left. Not a lot. Just a little. They walked all day, and the day after that, and the act of being his nightly sustenance kept her silent on his walking habits for longer than it should have. But then she caught a glimpse of strong, shaped wood on her left, through the trees and mud, in the distance, and she said to him, 'We're walking around in circles.'

'No,' he said, then, 'Are we?' not very believably at all, and she hated him and pitied him, and felt herself to be the stronger one, which was a powerful feeling, coursing through her. She thought she could get to love that feeling more than she loved him.

'It's fine,' she said tenderly, 'to be scared. But I guarantee you that you can walk on and out of this swamp and you will be fine. There's so much to see out there.'

'Like what?'

She told more stories, trying to keep to some touchstone of reality, about the horned road and the coast and the towns and the mountain chalet and the cha and the cave and the Spire of Telezon and the rockets to space. She found herself stressing the quest, the purpose of it, the way it united everything that had happened, would tie it all into a final knot at some point.

The First to Fall seemed more interested in the Spire than in her quest.

'I'd love to see one,' he said.

'They're not that great.'

'They are!' he said, and she suspected she had lost him, or had never really had him in the first place.

381

STILL, EVEN IF his love of the rockets would tear him away eventually, right now it kept him close, and he became obedient, tractable, if she said they were heading in that direction. Since Fairly had discovered she liked the feeling of being superior, she said it regularly.

'I can take you straight to them,' she said.

The First to Fall fixed his attention upon her squarely. 'Really?'

Could she? Could she backtrack, find her way back to the horned road and use it to return to where she'd started? She lied, and said, 'Absolutely,' and he hugged her, and praised her, and said, 'Where you walk, I will follow.'

The intoxicating feeling of it! To have his company, his servitude, his protection! The breathing man wouldn't stand a chance against them, united. She realised she hadn't caught a glimpse of him for an age. Perhaps they, together, had done what could not be done alone, or even by a stockade and a fleet of family: they had defeated him. *The power of love is strong*, she thought. She suspected she'd heard that line in a song, while pressing buttons on the jukebox in the town of Intervention. Strange, the things that had stayed with her.

She said, 'This way, this way,' and turned away from the distant line of the stockade. She led him in what she thought was a straight line, heading for whatever came next.

It didn't take long to emerge from the swamp, which turned out to be quite small, really, when not seen through unsure, directionless eyes. She simply followed the driest patches of land, never pressing back into mud, and in no time at all she had found a main road, a roaring tarmac slash through the land on which cars rushed by at ferocious speeds, all of them deafening and colourful and busy in their masses.

The First to Fall looked dumbstruck. He cringed away from each car that passed.

'It's okay,' said Fairly. 'It's just transport. Don't you have transport?'

'Only giant dogs with saddles on,' he said, and she felt maybe that was a step too far in terms of invention on his part, but she let it slide. She stuck out her thumb and the First to Fall tentatively followed suit.

IT TOOK A few minutes for a curved yellow camper van, big and jolly, to stop. The doors at the back were flung open and the passengers, sitting on two long benches on either side, were ready with smiles and sun-kissed complexions.

'Come on!' they said, 'Going your way!' and held out their hands. Fairly let them pull her in, and the First to Fall followed, and they all squeezed in together in the back of the van. The doors were pulled shut, and off they went.

The First to Fall, sitting opposite her and squeezed between two women no older than her, looked distinctly uncomfortable. Their thighs, in cut-off jeans shorts, pressed against him, and they examined him with intense interest.

Fairly felt for him. He had been a figure of royal privilege, a builder of a stockade, a leader. Now he was cramped in a van with no idea of where he was going. *How quickly life changes*, she thought, but then introductions were made and she put the thought aside so she could concentrate on everyone's names. Dan, Tracy, Jeff. Deep and Pinto. Trond in the driving seat. Gwen and Wing flanking the First to Fall.

'Where are you guys heading?' said Trond, who drove with one hand on the wheel and a lazy attention span for the road. He did not drive fast, and a regular stream of cars built up behind them. When they started honking he would stick one arm out of the window and wave them past, whether there was traffic in the incoming direction or not.

'The rockets!' said the First to Fall.

'Wherever's close,' said Fairly. 'If it's not too much trouble.'

'The more the merrier,' said Deep. 'You questers?'

The question struck her dumb for a moment.

'Only you've got the backpacks. We all decided to give up on that crap. Searching for our own truth now. The place we're going just happens to be on the horned road, so we're using it, but we're not slaves to it.'

'This is the horned road?' she asked.

'Yeah,' said Gwen, drawing out the word, making a face in amusement at her apparent stupidity.

But how could that be? The road was on a different land, wasn't it? Hadn't she left it behind?

381

'So WHERE ARE *you* going?' asked the First to Fall.

'It's sort of a secret,' said Pinto. He had a thin plaited rope between his fingers that he knotted and pulled, knotted and pulled. There was something unnerving about the way he leaned forward and spoke from the corner of his mouth.

'Well, if you could just drop us off at wherever's convenient,' she said, and the First to Fall shook his head.

'Rockets!' he said.

'Oh, just tell them,' said Trond, from the driver's seat. 'They're questers. They've probably worked it out anyway.'

Pinto threw Trond's back a disappointed look, but he began to speak, and he said:

Once upon a time an ancient and mystical civilization lived on this land and they were wise beyond measure, and knowledgeable beyond time. They were here waaaaay before we showed up. Some said they had, in fact, created humans. But then there were too many humans and the ancient ones began to die out. It wasn't even a war or a disease. It was just humans doing what they always do, and squeezing everything else out, absorbing them, leaving broken pieces of them scattered all over the place.

For a long time nobody even realised the ancient ones had been a really big deal. But then people began to look at the pieces left behind, and put some facts together. The pieces were small, left in plain sight. But people felt drawn to them when they felt sad, and everyone had started feeling really, really sad all the time because they were always being told where to walk and what to do.

And some people said—hey, those ancient ones

probably could have solved this problem of sadness! And other people laughed at them for saying it, but brave people, wise people, didn't listen to the laughter. They set up their own society, and they refused to do as they were told any more. They found each other and shared the pieces they'd found, and they were always out looking for new pieces.

But there was one piece that they were all certain of, and they shared that knowledge among themselves and cherished it. And that piece was made up of three words.

The words were simply:
COME
HERE
ALL
Get it?

381

'GET IT?' SAID Pinto. The others were all smiling at her with delight and enthusiasm.

'Get what?' she said.

'CHA!' said Pinto. 'It spells CHA!'

They all spoke over each other, then, hurrying to tell her all about the cha being the key to the past, present and future, being the ancient ones responsible for humanity itself, and how humans were the downfall of the magnificent cha, but cha had been there at the beginning and would be there at the end if only good humans could find all the pieces they'd left on this planet. Knowing about the cha was to set your feet on the path of the real quest, the important quest, of hunting for pieces. Everything else was, apparently, a total waste of time.

'Have you ever seen a cha?' asked Fairly.

'Nobody's seen one,' said Gwen. 'Nobody will until all the pieces are gathered.'

She thought of telling them all about her cha experiences, but decided against it.

'So we're seeking a piece,' said Tracy. 'We found a clue, and we're following it. Come with! It's going to be awesome.'

'Where did you learn all this?' said the First to Fall, awestruck. How easily he swallowed these ideas. All this talk of cha, and she was pretty certain she was the only one who had any actual experience in that department. She decided she'd fill in the truth for him later, when they were alone again, curled up tight within each other.

She took his hand and squeezed it, and the way he barely acknowledged that made her wonder if she would bother to tell him after all. Their relationship was hardly built on mutual honesty.

The ex-questers, lovers of the cha, talked on and on as the camper van ate up the road. By the end of the day, Fairly felt as if the First to Fall had become one of them. How quickly he had been subsumed into their ideas, without needing a shred of proof. He could repeat verbatim large sections of their cha mythology already, she suspected.

And why did she feel so distrustful of it? Wouldn't it be easier to go along with the flow? Couldn't they possibly be right?

She didn't know.

'It's good weather,' said Jeff. 'Let's sleep out.'

381

THEY PARKED IN a layby just off the horned road (if that was what it was) and made their way into a field of brilliant golden wheat. It was summer, Fairly realised. The night was balmy, beautiful. The First to Fall was still the most handsome body she had ever met, and that body wanted her body, and she gave herself over to that once more, not caring if the others heard them devouring each other under the stars.

Soon everyone was still, wrapped in their wheat beds, and she untangled herself from the First to Fall and headed for an open plain, hard tufted grass and the occasional thistle, to stare at the night. She wanted to be restless, accusatory. Her mind could not be still with all it had learned today.

She thought of the cha in the barn, pretending to be pigs, playing pigs' games.

She thought of the cha in the mountains, giving her access to their hot tub, and helping her until the moment of their massacre.

She thought of the roasted cha on the spit at the cave of teeth, and the way the smell had made her mouth water.

And she thought of the one cha token she still possessed, and the two tokens she had used as payment.

How were all these things connected? These facts, these moments, had to mean something.

It would be so easy to let go and believe their version of the world. The First to Fall had already done just that, so easily, without a qualm. And yet she could not manage it herself. And the more she stared at the stars and thought it through, the more it came to her that the reason for her reluctance lay with the breathing man.

He was still close by. Right now he felt ephemeral, abstract to her. But he would return to her reality. She did not want to forget him and be part of the great cha mystery instead. There didn't appear to be enough room within her for both.

Undecided, she sighed, and strode back to the others, taking care to avoid the prickly thistles. She lay down next to the First to Fall, let him roll over so his arm was across her middle, and slept.

SHE MOVED ONWARDS in the company of her lover and the ones who'd become her friends, even if she never did quite believe them. With each day that passed it became a little easier to say nothing in the face of their spiralling cha hunt, which she was certain would never resolve into anything. She wanted to belong to them, to fit with them, as the First to Fall had managed to do. They had given him a nickname—Foff—which he loved, and he had decided to try to learn all the old songs they would sing to him, repeating them over and over in the back of the campervan, bouncing along in time. All the songs were about open roads and love and long sunshine days.

'Where are you from?' she asked them, one day, thinking they might answer even if they wouldn't explain precisely where they were going. Tracy pointed at the road behind, and everyone joined in. Even Foff, and even Trond, who took both hands from the steering wheel to offer a two-thumbed response. How easy he found it to drive the van, casually, without fear even during the fast stretches, where they all seemed to be rushing into the future. She had been watching him closely, trying to get the knack of it.

'Want me to teach you?' Trond asked her, one night, over a meal of cold soup from dented cans retrieved from the boot, and she nodded. So he taught her to drive, and there certainly was a trick to it. Once she had it, it was easy as breathing. Arms and legs in rhythm, in movement, and the hands on the wheel, the eyes on the road. She loved to drive. They started taking it in turns. None of the others had any interest.

She wished she could share this new hobby with Foff, but he much preferred to sing with the others. They all agreed that he was, in fact, the best singer, and he wore this accolade with possessive delight. Could it be possible for the journey to go on together, she wondered? He as the best singer, and she as the co-driver, and they as lovers: a perfect ending that didn't end, the tension never growing, never fading away.

381

THEN SHE BEGAN to wonder: *Is the trick to life not to find the things you are looking for?*

A brown sign. Upon it: a white circle. No words.

'What does that mean?' said Fairly. She thought she'd learned all the signs of the road: *slower, faster, bends ahead*.

'I thought they were all gone,' said Trond, beside her, in the front passenger seat. He said he liked watching her drive as much as he liked to drive himself. They shared this love, for driving, for operating the campervan, and it was a pleasant feeling between them. But there was no more to it than that. Behind them, the others were singing one of Foff's many songs about swamps. They liked to belt them out at top volume in high, silly voices: *Swamps are good! Swamps are strong! In a swamp! We all belong!* She had begun to suspect they all liked him so much because he was so easy to make fun of, but she wouldn't tell him that.

'Gone? Why?'

Trond shrugged. 'A thing of the past, back when people were free and the cha kept us all safe. It's a tourist information board.'

'What's that?'

'It lets people know when there's something worth seeing. They were all over the place when I was growing up, and back then they pointed to things that weren't really of interest, like holes in the ground and buildings that had fallen down, so everyone gave up on them. This one must be left over.'

'Or maybe there really is something of interest there,' said Fairly.

'Like what?' said Trond, and another sign appeared, pointing to a gravel car park on the left. Fairly took the turn just as everyone's voices rose on the chorus, and shuddered—*woo woo woo swaaampp*, they sang, and then petered out as she parked up the van and spotted something ahead, something large jutting up from between hills in the dirt track. Two triangular points and a curve that joined them together, creating a shape Fairly felt she recognised. It was the very top of a head of a cha, surely. A huge cha. Well, maybe not huge compared to the tallest buildings of Telezon, but out here in the middle of nowhere, it dwarfed the landscape.

381

THEY ALL GOT out of the campervan and walked, crept, down the path. Something about the cha called for respect, for an obsequious approach, even though she knew it was a statue. There could be no doubt about it. It was perfectly still. Not lifelike at all. The closer they got, the more it revealed itself to be a not very good statue. It emerged from the rock face, erect, on two legs, its head thrown back to the sky. She had never seen a cha in such a pose; she felt it captured no recognisable aspect of cha personality. How solemn it looked, and unfriendly. It had giant testicles, great balls on display, and a slightly open mouth exposed a row of jagged teeth.

No matter what level of skill had been involved in capturing its form, it did retain a more than impressive quality simply for the scale of it. They reached it to find their heads level with its knees, and they looked up at it in silence.

Fairly reached out a hand.

'Don't,' said Foff, quiet, aghast, so she dropped her hand back to her side and walked as far around the statue as she could, to the place where the rock became the beginning of the statue. There was no way to complete a full circle of it. There were no signs, no statements as to what it meant or who had sculpted it. And yet she felt the others breathe differently in its presence, and settle into the awe that came from validation. *We were right*, their breaths said, even and slow. Why else would such a monument exist? It must have come from the past, the time of the cha ruling the world wisely and well, and helping the poor little humans to find their destinies.

But the statue did not look old to Fairly. It looked new. No lichen had made their home upon it, no weathering of the rock had occurred. The quality of the work was even, if not accurate. She suspected that it had been made quickly, roughly, by machine.

Tracy sat at its feet and the others followed suit. 'Let's stay here,' she said with reverence, certainty. 'Let's sing our songs to it. It needs to hear our voices.'

381

EVERYONE WAS DELIGHTED to stay, and stay, and stay some more. The hours passed. Songs were sung.

Fairly tried hard not to feel differently. She wished she

hadn't noticed that the statue looked new and sloppy. Things only got worse when she found the join.

'Look,' she said, on day eight of singing around the cha statue. 'Right here. Right under the testicles. The legs are joined to the body there. The parts were made separately elsewhere, and then attached to the rock here. It's not even part of the cliff, really. Look. The stone is a slightly different colour.'

'I can't see it,' said Trond. Without driving in common, he had drifted away, become less inclined to listen to her. Their friendship had been fickle, after all.

The others agreed, and Foff said, 'Silly,' to her, in an affectionate tone of voice. Lately he had been using that tone more and more—reversing the direction in which their relationship had previously flowed. It felt like a belittlement, which made Fairly feel bad about her own behaviour. Things had to move away from that guilt; she had to make it move.

The hot, dry weather never changed out here, under the cha statue, but love did.

That night, lying under the stars, Fairly woke Foff by sliding her hand into his underwear. When she had his attention she whispered, 'Don't you still want to see the rockets?'

'Yeah,' he whispered back, although she suspected he would have agreed to anything at that moment.

'We should go. Find the rockets.'

'What's the rush?'

What was her rush?

Standing still was her rush. Strange stories about cha were her rush. The breathing man, and all the places she'd been, and all the things she still had to do were her rush. *Her* quest. Not his. Hers.

She couldn't stay, but she struggled to leave. She had merged into them, somehow, even as the lesser one, the last one.

But she knew, deep down, that the cha statue had a join, and so did she.

To belong was an excruciating, sticky demand on one used to separation. Fairly, with every passing day, no longer wanted to feel that she was lost in a halfway place, caught somewhere between the act of rejecting and belonging.

381

HADN'T EVERY SONG been learned and sung, she wondered, while they sang around the statue? Swamps and cha and other musical stories. She wondered if Foff even remembered the swamp. She said to him, while they were picking berries from the plenteous bushes nearby, 'Don't you miss your brothers?'

He thought about it, and said, 'Sure. This is important, though, don't you think?'

'More important than family?'

He stared at her. 'Isn't this our family now? Aren't you my family?'

Enough, she thought.

The next morning she woke and cried out, 'I've had an epiphany!'

They were the kind of family who were into epiphanies, so they all gathered round, and she told them of her own experience with the cha, including the spit and the hot tub, but she framed it as a mystical vision. Using her own past, she pulled a thread of silvery truth through her words, and that gave her confidence. 'So you see,' she said, as she reached the end, 'we need to find the mountain chalet of the cha and help them. We need to stop them from being hunted and eaten.'

'Isn't the statue important?' said Deep. 'Doesn't it prove we're right?'

'It's a sign,' said Fairly.

The others all nodded.

In no time at all they were back in the camper van and Fairly let Trond drive the first leg to give him a sense of purpose.

'Let's go!' she said. 'It's this way.' The direction of the road, of course. What other way was there to go? She feigned certainty, and hoped that over time they'd all simply trust in her apparent sense of direction and forget to wonder over the story she'd told them which was half the truth and some personal gain mixed in. Still, the relief of no longer being stuck at the statue overpowered her guilt, and kept her going.

But they did not forget. They kept asking her questions about the vision she'd had, and she kept telling them, and they wanted more and more. *What did it all mean?* they said. *What exactly could it mean?* And the horned road was not like it was before; after a few miles it petered out into rocks and grass, and was no longer suitable for vehicles at all.

381

'You MUST HAVE led us in the wrong direction,' said Trond, who seemed to be cultivating an active dislike of her now, even though they had driving in common again.

'No, no,' she said. 'It's this way.'

'Maybe you just missed a turn. We should turn around, head back a little way.'

'It's this way,' she repeated.

'You sure?'

'Absolutely.'

They drove on in silence. The road was too bumpy for singing; it made their voices wobble.

The rocks and grass gave way to mud.

And the camper van stuck there, in the mud, wheels spinning, clods of brown muck coating the sides. Trond tried reversing. There was only the sound of the engine struggling, the wheels whizzing. He turned off the engine, and everyone looked at her.

'Are you making this shit up?' said Tracy.

'I'm not!' she said, but the ring of truth had left her, along with all her confidence. They groaned as one and got out of the van, and threw down rocks so the wheels could, at least, reverse to relative stability. Then they all returned to the camper van, except for Fairly, who stood disconsolately by the big back door.

'We'll go back to the statue,' said Trond.

'No!' Fairly shouted. Backwards was not an option. She knew it as she shouted, and it became clear to her, as it never had before, that the cha statue was some sort of trap for those who could not get past it, and it had something to do with the devices and the breathing man. She had things to do, a quest to complete, and other experiences to have. New loves lay ahead of her. She didn't need this old one anymore.

She prepared herself for a fight. Let them say whatever, let them hate her and try to persuade her, but she knew she had to go on, and—

'Bye,' said Foff. He chucked her backpack out of the window. Trond started the van and they reversed away. She could hear them starting up a song as they went. Then Trond did a neat three-point turn on the grass, and they sped up, and were gone.

Fairly watched them drive away.

Right then.

She faced the mud ahead.

The other direction would certainly have been easier.

381

She started walking and the mud sucked at her feet. It wanted to dirty her, unbalance her. It wanted her to lie down in it. She kept going for what felt like the longest time of her life. Longer, even, than waiting around by that stupid statue. Feelings she had not experienced since meeting the First to Fall—she could stop calling him Foff, now, at least, which was a ridiculous name—began to return to her. How could she have forgotten what it felt like to be alone?

Some decisions, once made, are made forever.[58]

Or they feel like forever, which is no different, in the moment of realisation.

Through the mud, stumbling on. Was this even a road at all? Only the faintest trail of stones kept her moving. Love, or whatever it had been, was left behind.

Up ahead, coalescing below gathering grey clouds on the flat horizon, was an object.

The object was shaped just like a chain device.

For a long time, during the stumble to it, she did not

---

58 I'm back.

allow herself to believe that it could be a real device. It had to be a dummy, a fake, another trap. It was only when she reached it that she allowed herself to be persuaded that she had been travelling in the right direction all along— the device proved it. It was part of the quest. And this was the end of some part of the quest, even though the way looked the same before and after. It was the end of… love. No. She was certain that it hadn't been love after all, not with the First to Fall, not with Fortune. The end of self-deception? She hoped so. No more cha, maybe. No more breathing man. She found she wished for those things fervently. Who would she become without them?

This was the end of something. And after an end came a beginning.

A beginning that meant she had to find the will to keep travelling.

She put her hand to the button, but did not press it. Not yet. The sun began to set. The clouds came to her, and a light rain began falling upon her. The mud cooled as it slipped over her shoes and through her socks.

381

THE CHAIN DEVICE was just like the others: a solid silver box with a big red button on top.

Round and round in circles went Fairly's thoughts. It was suddenly so important to try to think clearly, to escape these cycles of adventure, of journey, of recommencement. But she couldn't; could she come to accept that? That she would always be Fairly, no matter what, no matter where it took her next and how she looked upon it, no matter if she was at the beginning, the end, or the middle, she was still Fairly, Fairly, always just Fairly—

She pressed the button, in desperation, in delight, and for a moment it seemed that nothing has happened, would happen, is happening. Then it dawns on me. I am here. I am present, alive, in this moment. I have survived some things, and will survive others. For the first time, I understand the pleasure I can take in being alone, having my own thoughts, making my own path. And it does not have to be the horned road.

I rest my hand on the depressed button. A slight vibration comes from the device. It's audible, I realise. A very low hum. I can't remember hearing it at the other devices, although perhaps I was not really paying attention. Not like I am now, living in heightened awareness of self.

What does the button do?[59]

---

59 Twenty or so pages and fifty-two years later, I'm surprised to find myself looking at this dance again. How strange to pick it up once more! To push the button, one might say. Meanwhile I've been off living my life, and it was nothing like I thought it would be. I was so certain that

I picture a line, an electrical wire, that runs from the bottom of the button, within the device, to the ground. Then deep down into the mud. Then further. To a place where all buttons are linked.

I feel powerful with possibility.

I find I want to know what all these buttons do. How do they work? Is this science, or art, or magic? Are there trained cha on treadmills, strapped inside, or a wise talking cha waiting to be found?

The hum intensifies.

It turns into shaking: a loud, teeth-rattling experience, and the casing around the button clatters, and one corner pops free of its fixings.

The hum stops.

I put my finger to the open corner, and pull.

---

being a historian was my destiny. I wanted very badly to have something to offer to that ongoing process. I saw it as the pinnacle of our society, but here's the thing – for many of us it's not even an issue. They take it for granted that others will be holding all the correct information in the correct way for them, and once I realised that it was okay to be that kind of person I was transformed. It took years. It didn't come naturally to me at all. Fairly's narrative was the catalyst. Her story made me realise that it's acceptable to be on the outskirts of meaning. It's all an illusion of control anyway. The more I thought of Fairly, struggling to make sense of it all, the more I came to see that whether she understands the world she lives in is irrelevant.

Here's the thing – Fairly's journey never was about me.

The casing comes off, easily, and I see—nothing. There's nothing inside. No, wait. There's a hole in the ground that drops away into the depths of darkness.

381

I PUT MY head into the device and call into the hole.

'Hello?'

I feel like it's listening to me, even as I listen to it.

A voice comes to me. I don't catch what it says. It floats up, soft, from the hole, and maybe it's not even a word. Maybe it's a sound. Not from a person, but from an animal. Or from the landscape. I look up, wondering if the sound came from the hole at all, or from the mud around me, and I see the breathing man.

The breathing man is here.

He approaches.

He walks quickly over the mud as if it doesn't bother him, can't stick to him. He is moving fast. I have no time to make decisions.

He took me, before, and sailed away with me. He made me stand so close. He breathed on me. He watched me. He had me in his grip; how did I escape him? I don't know. I can't remember. I must escape him again.

Through the hole.

I can't outrun him. There is only the hole. It will fit me, I think. It will be very tight, but I can make it. I take off my backpack and hold it in my hands. Hands first into the hole. Then head. My shoulders fit inside. It is so dark in here. It is insane, headfirst into the dark, I will die, I will die. Tight on my hips, but there's room, my weight is tipped. I will fall. I never should have left the van. Where is the First to Fall? He would have kept the breathing man at bay. I should have stayed with his brothers, been happy, been safe, why can't I be happy and safe? I call down the hole, 'Help!' The breathing man must be nearly upon me. I can't bear to look upon him again. I would rather—I would rather—My face is cold. I will fall. 'Help!' I say. 'Help!'

I fall.

I fall for a moment, and the slippery sides of the hole are a metal tube that holds me, elongates with me, and I slide, slide along and down, along and down. Like a ride. I can't stop myself. I am only along for the ride.

381

THE RIDE DOESN'T last long.[60] It's just long enough to

60 Having said that, I've decided to revisit this document one last time, and make it all about me, in the sense that my interpretation matters – to me, at least! I want to finish what I started. Because – and here's what I've really come to understand by abandoning the very principles of my age – society isn't only for the people who have something to contribute. It also must be for everyone who

make me feel I am gaining distance, escaping him. Then it widens, and slows, and there is light. I can't see where this yellow glow is coming from. The final yards of the tunnel slope to an opening, and I put my feet on a road once more. The road runs underground, and I am at a crossroads. Each direction leads to another well-let walkway. North, south, east, west? Possibly. It looks like an awesome accomplishment of engineering, to rival the spire and the rockets, and for the first time I think: *who is building all this stuff?* It's not anyone from my village, which is filled with solid workers, without inspiration. It's not the people I've met along the horned road, who were working in the tourist industry or were tourists. It's not me. I was never even offered the opportunity to learn how to make such a thing, and perhaps I would have liked to try.

This land is built by others, and it is not for me.

---

can't or won't contribute. It's a set of demands placed by some upon others. Dr Magnaman set out his parameters, but the more I travelled, the more I realised that those guidelines seemed ridiculous, nonsensical, to others, *even as they reaped the benefits!* To cherish the individual, even the idiosyncratic, is to place value on participation, not capability, and not understanding. Life experience has shown me that. I'm no historian, never was, and yet here I am doing it! At age 69, two months before my death, I choose to spend my time doing something I'm no good at.

The road is a glimpse of this land, and no more, and I have not seen enough to know what it means. Not to even speculate.

I'm being asked to make a meaningless choice, and once I have chosen I will blame myself for whatever comes next. *I made the wrong choice*, I'll say to myself, in the aftermath of whatever crap comes next.

And none of this changes the fact that the breathing man is on his way here right now. Could he fit down the hole?

I will move.

I will operate on the feeling that one way is back and the other way is forward. I turn in a circle until I stop, and go forward.

Here I go.

If it's wrong, it's wrong.

I trot along the walkway in the yellow glow from nowhere.

After a while I look over my shoulder and see—nothing. He is not following me, at least, not as far as I can see. And another strange thing—I leave no footprints. Not a mark. The floor is tacky underfoot, maybe some kind of plastic. I can move without changing the landscape. He won't be able to see which way I've gone.[61]

---

61 Look at me, writing away like not a day went by. This is amazing. It turns out I had really deep thoughts while I was off being a hedonist. Nothing ever leaves you, really, does

381

THAT'S GOOD, BUT this walkway is so long and straight, and I can still see the crossroads—and the lip of the tunnel above it—in the distance. I must get out of sight somehow. Where is a turning? I break into a run, then up it to a sprint. I give it everything: my breath, my muscles, my will to be far away, and when I am finally forced to slow, my blood and lungs singing, I look back and find I can no longer see the crossroads.

I stop.

I listen. I listen hard.

I hear footsteps.

I listen for a time, and it seems to me they are receding.

I hope they are receding.

If I start running again, my own footsteps will be loud, and the breathing man will follow the sound. Is that a thing that could happen? I could bring my own destruction upon me.

This, this choice. This agony of paralysis, this second in which I might save myself or damn myself—this, over and over again—this is life. This is my life.

I can't go on.

I have to.

---

it? Revelations like these are all part of getting older. I still maintain that living in the ageing body has much to offer. Never mind.

The footsteps.

They are receding.

Surely they are dying away.

Yes, they are quieter. I'm certain. It's only that I'm listening so hard; if I wasn't straining to catch them, I would not be able to hear them at all.

I place my foot gently, no sound, and then I transfer my weight, and then I move the other. I repeat. I repeat. I am moving away from him, and from that feeling. I can go on. I lied to myself, back there, ten steps ago. That despair was a lie. I can't be trusted. Or maybe it was the truth back then.

Silent steps, taking me in a direction I have never been before.

The walkway does not deviate, bears no markings, for the longest time. But that's good. It means definite progress. I can't be doubling back. One way, one path. The feeling of eyes on the back of my neck will pass; I turn again and again and never see him. He can't be invisible, can he? *Get a grip*, I tell myself.

The phrase is calming.

Then: a small sign hanging from the ceiling.

It reads:

KEN'S SNACK SHACK[62]

---

62 I had a hole inside me. That's what happened. A big hole where something satisfying should be. Something I

381

DO SIGNS ALWAYS lead somewhere? Can there be signs without outcomes?

There's faith in a sign, unspoken, and I fall for it this time, just as I have all the other times. Ken's Snack Shack, up ahead. I believe it. But for the first time I wonder:

Who leaves the signs?

Who is in charge of sign-making?[63]

There's no way to answer this, and I'm not expecting Ken—whoever he is—to have an answer either, but he might have a snack, at least, and I am hungry for something other than my own supplies. And thirsty for anything but water. And worn down to a nub by this game of hide and seek, running and running. So I follow the sign, even though it's in the only direction, the exact direction, I was going anyway, and soon I see the walkway widening up ahead, expanding to create another crossroads, and in the centre of that crossroads, a hut.

---

couldn't get from reading and commenting on the past. I used to feel like such a fraud. I remember sitting there, staring out of the view of my bedroom window, listening to my mother trying out some new recipe in the kitchen downstairs, enjoying the use of her arms, and I was thinking: *I'm a fraud. I'm making a terrible job of being a person.* Ha! Not half as bad as I'm making now. And I don't even care.

63 Okay, I do care a little bit.

The hut is made of wood, and the roof is conical, piles of straw stacked to a point that nearly touches the ceiling. I soon discern a large 'K' painted on the straw in black; no doubt if I moved around the shack I would find a matching 'E' and 'N' following on.

And I see Ken.

I assume it's Ken.

He's standing in his shack. The sides are open from waist height; below that, the walls are shelves, stocked with brightly coloured packets. He spies me, and waves, and I speed up and reach his bald head, his big smile, his large arms and assessing, blatant gaze. I like him.

'A hungry quester!' he says. 'At the end of their magnificent journey.'

At the end?

He holds up one finger and stops the question before I can ask it.

'You're all the same,' he says, with good humour. 'Always surprised to find you've reached the end. Because this is it. The last device is just up there.' He turns his finger to point to a branch of the crossroads. I can see a metal ladder that has been drilled to the shiny wall. It leads up to a hatch. 'Always the same questions, too. You're adorable. The backpack. The bemused look. Our fine future,' he says. 'Yes. Our fine, fine future.'

381

'HOW MANY QUESTERS?' I ask him.[64]

'You mean, how many a week? Maybe five.'

'Five a week?'

'For the past few years. I don't know about before then—that's when I bought the business. Want chocolate?' He hands me a wrapped bar. I rip it open and eat it so fast, creamy brown chocolate; I barely even taste it properly, and he smiles and hands me another one before I've even finished the first.

'What about the breathing man?' I ask.

'Who?'

'The man who's been following me. Was he part of the quest?'

'Oh him. Don't worry. That's all over with.'

Such relief. The second bar, I taste. Milk chocolate and nuts. My favourite. I am a girl again, treated, cossetted, on a trip to the city. Fattened up for this game, this endless conveyor belt of questers. I am—we are—apparently so predictable. Everything that has happened to me has not

---

64 Here's what happened: I gave up on trying to explain or understand Fairly's quest, and it affected me deeply. I didn't know where to go, what to do with my life. I looked at other people my age, signing up for their futures, looked at myself and saw only that big hole. But where there are holes, things rush in. And the thing that rushed into my hole was the Department of Lived Experience.

even been interesting; at least, not to anyone but me, who took it for unique because I knew no better.

Even though I feel devalued, cheapened, I can't help myself. When smiling Ken passes me a third bar of chocolate, I eat it. Then, full of chocolate, the wrappers crumpled in my hand, I thank him. And he says, 'Don't thank the man, just pay the man! It's a cha.'

'A cha?'

'You know, every quester gets three. And every quester has one left at this point. It's no good to you anymore. Worthless, beyond the final device. So the price is a cha, and cheap at that, too.' He reaches under the counter and brings up a great handful of cha, the shiny decorated solid objects. Together, nestled in his palm, they look of little value.

I reach into my backpack and bring out my final cha. I put it in his palm, with the others.

'That'll do nicely,' he says, and it's the words, rather than the act of giving, that makes me feel uncomfortable, as if I have failed some final test. Betrayed the cha, somehow, even though it's only a painted pebble, isn't it? They were only ever painted pebbles, really.

'Have one more on the house,' Ken says.

So I take one more bar, and pocket it, and I say, 'Thank you.'

381

'OFF YOU GO, then. Up the ladder. Last one. Well done. You know, you remind me of my daughter.'

'Did she do the quest?' I ask him.

'Goodness, no, no, I wouldn't put her through that nonsense. She works in town, for the—you know.' He puts his hands to his temples. Are those triangles he's making, with his fingers? 'It's a good job,' he says, defensively, then points to the ladder once more. I cross to it, and climb it, a rung at a time into the light once more, and I find myself in a flowered meadow, poppies and daisies knee high, where the final device can be found.

It looks just like the others. It's connected to the others. But what connects it? Only air. Are they communicating? Are there things about the devices that I cannot see?

Well, I can see this device very clearly, and the big red button, and I can see the field with the buttercups and dandelions, and the bright blue sky above. It's a good place to end a quest, isn't it? As good as any.

I take my time sauntering to the device. Free of the breathing man, I will not rush this conclusion. I count slow breaths and enjoy the feeling of space inside me. Pre-emptive emptiness? Or perhaps it's the lightness of my pocket after spending my final cha. Those small pebbles were heavier than I thought.

But the lightness, the ease—I think maybe that's within me, too. No more marching around the world, trying to follow the horned road to its conclusion. I will make my own path, wherever it leads. I feel freer. More adult. More careful in my thoughts, and quieter, if that's maturity. I hope that's maturity. I have been taught! I have become my potential.

And once the button is pressed, I will feel something else again.

I will feel—

There.

Pressed.

At first, nothing happened. At least, it seemed that way, for the things I was expecting to happen—completion, contentment, conclusion—did not come to me instantly. I was just the same. Well. No. Not quite. I was wiser. I knew then, for certain, that the devices really did do something.

This one summoned a cha in a hot air balloon.[65]

---

65 The Department of Lived Experience came into my life like a giant colourful gift, and I will forever be grateful for that. A flyer. A big flyer pinned to my streamboard, glowing and shimmying and looking very different from all the other notices. It said:

THIS IS NOT AN IMPORTANT MESSAGE
But it might be a fun one

It went on to tell me that I didn't have to make a difference. I didn't have to add my thoughts to others. I didn't need to make sense of it all. Then it mentioned a room, and a

381

AT FIRST I saw it as only a dot, a faraway punctuation mark in the sky, but as it got closer it filled out into a bubble, and I saw the basket underneath, and I began to hear the creaking of the basket swaying in the wind and there it was—a cha. In the basket. I made out the fur of its round face and the triangular ears. It was larger than any I had come across before. Human-sized.

At that point I realised it was a human. A human in a costume of a cha. It was a strange moment, made from seeing the head turn oddly on the body, and the way the neck was held. Yes, a mask of a cha over a person, and after the balloon landed, not far from the device, squashing the flowers of the field flat, the woman in the basket took off her cha head, tucked it under her arm, and beckoned me over.

'Well done,' she said. 'This must all come as a bit of a shock. The end of the quest! It takes a bit of getting used to for everyone. You're not unusual. Take your time, and breathe. I had a fainter once. If you feel funny, have a sit down. No rush.' She checked her wristwatch.

'I don't understand.'

'Sure! Sure. Me neither, really. I'm only doing my job. I

---

time, in my old socialisation classroom, and I went along, wondering what I was doing. It turned out I was making the best decision of my life.

don't have any more information to give you.' She had a pleasant, if nervous smile. I got the feeling she was being paid by the hour. 'They said: be honest. So, here's the truth, I don't know anything. I got paid and I'm here, right on time. You pressed the button. Voilà. I'm Angie.'

'Fairly,' I said. 'You can call me Fair.' I don't know why I said that. Nobody, before or after that moment, ever called me Fair.

'I'm meant to give you a lift,' she said.

Angie was a little older than me, but not by much, and I thought she acted a little like I would have, in the circumstances.

'To where?'

'CHQ. Cha Headquarters.' She put her cha head back on and pointed fingers at herself, the end of her cha nose, as if it meant something. And I realised it probably did.

381

I WANTED TO help her get her job done. That was the reason I got into the balloon, even though the idea of it scared me. But I've been forever glad that I did. It was an unforgettable experience, and I consider myself lucky to have been there, high in the sky, breathing in the air, sharp and brittle in my lungs, my stiff fingers sinking into the lip of the basket. And the land changed underneath me, expanded, formed into one creature of rolls and plunges,

lines and spirals, to which everything, every experience
I had undergone, belonged. I recognised nothing in
particular, but felt like a part of it all.

Also, there was real panic, as I discovered I didn't really
care for heights.[66] It's a blessing to feel such panic, to
recognise the precarious nature of life. Of course, it did

---

66 I turned up, and I was the only person there. Nobody
else had time for such frivolity, perhaps. I was totally
alone. I waited. And waited. Then, out of the blue, a
person. A tall, friendly person wearing a jaunty yellow
cap, and he said to me, 'You're perfect. Follow me.' Have
you ever been told you're perfect, as a body, as a soul?
It's powerful stuff. I followed him out of the building, all
the way through the campus to the tramline, and we
went to the seaport, where the *Commitment to Frivolity*
awaited me. It was a beautiful boat, gleaming and low
in the water, a flag on the mast bearing the university
colours. I lost my heart to it at once, and I signed on to
become one of the crew – the cook! I knew a little about
cooking from my mother's efforts, but still. Ridiculous. I
know what you're thinking – you're thinking: *This is just
like Fairly's adventure! Off in a camper van, with a heap
of drop-outs!* Not at all. This was an academic project to
see if it could be ascertained how life can be measured in
terms of deliberately obtuse parameters. Fun. Success.
Experience. Love. You may argue that it's an impossible
task to measure organic life in that way, to which the
captain of the *Commitment to Frivolity* (my yellow-capped
warrior) would say, 'Then why are you already trying?'
He's not wrong, is he? Pretending not to care about
something is not the same as deciding to be free of it.

not feel that way at the time. I was beside myself with painful exhilaration, and I wanted it to stop. I'm only glad that it didn't.

Angie was good enough to ignore my silent tears, my grimacing face. She breathed deeply for both of us, beat on her chest with her fists, and said things like, 'Ahhhh!' and 'Bracing!' She pointed things out: places I had never heard of. 'That's the Bomonton Estuary,' she said, and, 'Oh look! The Manic Desert of Gorsht.' Or maybe I misheard. It wasn't until the city came into sight, that city with its central spire and the promise of rockets to space, that I felt a jolt of recognition for a place I'd been before.

'Telezon,' she said.

Complex feelings arose in me. I had lived with the strongest feelings that I should forever be moving onwards, down the road, not returning to some location that I had imagined far behind. It turned out it had only been a short ride away all the time.

But since I was not technically on a quest any longer, what difference could it make? And it was close to home, too. I remembered home, my mother, with sudden telescopic fondness, as if seeing them from very far away. It was easier to love them from that angle. I was on the cusp of returning to them, if that was what I decided to do.

381

THEN I REMEMBERED the person I had been on that first night in Telezon, finding myself a room, trying to gather my thoughts, finding my way through a task that seemed too huge to conquer:

Complete a Quest.

It turned out completing the quest had not been so very hard after all, not really. Or perhaps that was only the business of looking back, not forward. *The way always has seemed clearer when one turns to see that old obstacles have been overcome.* I think my mother said that down the chime to some poor nameless quester, once.

The Spire! It grew taller and taller as we travelled towards it. I found I wanted to return to it. Would the First to Fall be there, perhaps? Would he have found his way to that embarkation point? I wanted to stand outside the Spire… Well, not stand there, waiting, but be on my way to some other location, with a purposeful but not hurried step, and see him, come across him, and slow, and say hi, and be cool and suave and disinterestedly pleased to have found him. Or for him to have found me. Yes. And then I could make him feel bad for abandoning me. Not that I cared.

My quest? I would say. *Why, yes, I have finished that. It was very rewarding.*

Come with you? I would say. *Into space? Yes, why not?* Or possibly, *No, no, I have my own plans. I'm my own woman now.* Either. I rehearsed both as the balloon came into land.

We slowly deflated to the ground, between the buildings, and landed in an enclosed, deserted square, not far from the Spire. I was amazed by the emptiness, but Angela pointed out a sign on the wall:

LANDING AREA CHA-8
TO BE KEPT CLEAR AT ALL TIMES

Two men in overalls emerged from a door a little way along the wall, and industriously began to tether the balloon to the ground.

'Three minutes,' one of them said to Angie.

'What?' she cried, as if personally injured.

'Make it five, then,' he said.

'What's happening?' I asked her.

'I've got five minutes to have a pee and eat a sandwich,' she said. 'It was lovely meeting you.' She climbed out of the basket.

381

'WAIT—IS THAT it? What now?'

She pointed to another arrow-shaped sign, on the opposite wall. It was too far away for me to read, so I climbed from the basket and crossed to it.

WAITING AREA CHA-8
TO BE OCCUPIED BY AT LEAST
ONE QUESTER AT ALL TIMES

I turned back to Angela, but she was gone.

I decided then and there that, whatever came next, I didn't want to work for any company that gave an employee only five minutes for lunch and a pee as if that was a blessing. But what, then? What could I do with the rest of my life?

There was only one immediate answer: follow the arrow.[67]

So I did.

---

67 The first place we went was the Unity Spire, and you know what? It was spectacular. Particularly from the water. It really is very big. It's also really ugly. I wasn't expecting that. Up close you can see it's made of rough, jumbled shapes that don't really fit together very well, but what can you expect when it was made by so many different people? Each body that comes to an end donates some small object to add to the spire, and somehow they all hang together to create a decorated hub of all knowledge.

It reminded me of Fairly, looking up at that spire, just as she had stared up at the Spire in Telezon, and I realised I couldn't return and pick up my life once more. No more interpretation for me: only experience.

I said to my captain, 'Do we have to go back?' and the captain said, 'No!'

Even though it occurred to me that I really couldn't be called any sort of hero for completing a quest that was so well signposted. It turned out I was only one small cog in a vast machine of questers so predictable that we could be timetabled to arrive at the final point every few minutes. Quester: what did the word even mean? It was their word for me, for adventuring forth, for trying to do the right thing.

Their.

Who were *they*?

I felt odd, vulnerable. Exposed. I followed the arrow anyway, because there is comfort in following things, and it led to a glass door, and beyond that, a cool white space, plastic chairs and one low table in the centre, and a vending machine for snacks and drinks in one corner, next to a blue painted door that was firmly shut. It reminded me of the doctor's surgery I had once visited in Telezon. It seemed all waiting areas looked alike, or maybe they held the same feeling, of time unavoidably misspent, of chances not taken to be elsewhere. It was a sad room, and it contained only one other person: a boy about my age. Or should I say he was a man? I would have wanted to be called a woman. An adult. He was an adult, of roughly my age, and he glanced at me as I entered, then deliberately steered his gaze away, to a picture on the wall opposite the seat he had taken. It was a picture of a clouded blue sky.

I DIDN'T SPEAK to him and he didn't speak to me.

I took a seat at an angle to his own, banging my shins on the low table in the process. He had a backpack still on his back; he had to lean forward in the chair a little. I did the same thing. I didn't want to remove the backpack. And our hands, twitching in our laps, were the same. We were the same.

There was so much I wanted to ask him, to know about his quest, but since we had started in silence I found it impossible to speak. Instead I tried to transmit to him psychically.

Please, I willed him. *Please. Speak.*

Please.

With every minute that passed it was less possible to talk.

I shifted in my plastic seat, and he shifted in his. His seat made a high, thin sound like a fart; his face changed immediately, the cheeks drawing in, the mouth painfully tight in abject embarrassment. The urge to laugh came over me and I fought it ferociously, aghast, until it was defeated.

But the fake-fart had broken the silence.

I remembered how I'd walked miles, caved and nearly drowned and mountaineered and sung in camper vans and been abducted and pressed a lot of buttons, and I said, 'I—er—I just arrived and I was wondering if you—'

The blue door opened.

A businesslike voice called out, 'Next.'

'Sorry,' said the boy man adult. He got up with care, his hands on the sides of the seat—to avoid the repetition of the embarrassing sound, I suppose—and left the room.

Opportunity missed.

I should have learned from it. I don't think I ever have.

There was, at least, the vending machine. And it was free: no requests for cha I no longer had to spend. I dispensed a lukewarm cup of coffee, and chose a packet of three biscuits, arranged in a row in clear plastic, from the goods on display. They tumbled from their holding place when I pressed in the number, and broke into pieces. I ate the larger pieces, dipping the tiny, cracked edges into the coffee, thinking about vegetables. When did I last have a vegetable? Wasn't healthy eating any sort of priority for questers?

381

WHO WAS RESPONSIBLE for our basic needs, like toiletries and vitamins?[68] I had assumed I had to think about all

----

68 We came together as a crew, joined by our mutual experiences. We sailed our way around this beautiful planet of ours. It's not the Age of Curation. It's the Age of Elation. It offers opportunities galore. Toiletries and vitamins – hah! Packing accordingly. Did I care about things like that? I

those things for myself, and to moan about it would be more childlike than adult. But, in that waiting room, I realised that whoever was in charge was happy to give orders about the issues that mattered to them, and had no interest in what mattered to me.

Maybe the mark of true adulthood is the ability to moan.

On the wall next to the blue door, a framed painting of grey and black strokes, a jumble, caught my eye. I stared at it for a while. The more I looked at it, the more obvious it became to me that it represented the head of a cha, in three-quarter profile, one eye watching me back.

The main door opened behind me. An old woman entered. She moved with difficulty, as if every part of her had had enough of living, and then she stopped and rubbed one hip. 'Finally,' she said. She smiled at me as she lowered herself into a plastic chair with an exhalation of breath. I noticed she, too, wore a backpack that stopped her from leaning back in the seat.

I have no idea why, but her age made her easy to speak to. 'Shall I get you a coffee?' I said, quite loudly. I found I did not want to know anything about her. If she had

---

can't remember. I don't think so, not once I got the hang of being myself. I might have taken a vitamin or two from the regular bodycare package I got sent, but it certainly wasn't my priority. Once you've accepted you have a body you sort of have to forget about it.

been on a quest all this time, throughout her whole life, it would have been too much for me. Unbearable. I felt profoundly lucky, for a moment. This was an end. The end.

She nodded. I got her a coffee.

She sipped it.

'Did you…' she said tentatively, and at that moment the blue door opened.

'Next,' said the argument-proof voice.

'Bye,' I said, an apology disguised in a farewell, and then I did as I was told. I went through the door, down a white corridor, so plain it almost hurt, and followed it until it widened. An archway admitted me to a long room. Ornate tapestries lined the walls, and a vast fire was burning under a stone mantelpiece. At the far end of the room, at a heavy table with curved legs, sat three cha.

381

NOT CHA. PEOPLE wearing cha heads.

I stood at the back of the room, feeling the heat of the great fire. It was unbearably warm, and the tapestries were vivid, showing scenes of cha as gods, as demons, as angels, arranged in artful poses. I wondered if I was feverish. I put a hand to my forehead and found it cool. The people in cha costumes seemed to take it as a greeting. One beckoned me forward. Another said, 'Draw closer, quester, and stand before us.'

I did as I was told.

The central cha-dressed person was bigger than the two flanking him; it had to be a large man under the mask. He wore a white shirt with a pointed collar that accentuated the small triangular ears on the top of the cha mask.

The heat of the fire was ferocious.

'Congratulations on completing the quest,' said the central man. He had a sonorous voice; it filled the room.

'Thank you,' I said.

'What do you think?'

'I—I think I'm—thank you.'

'No, no,' he said. 'About cha. What do you think about cha?'

'They're...' I thought hard for something meaningful to say, and settled for, '...everywhere.'

'Yes they are. And what does that tell you?'

'They can be helpful,' I said.

Was it my imagination, or did all three of them lean forward? I felt I was the centre of their intense focus.

'Go on,' said the central man.

'But most people don't really know that.'

'And what does that tell you?'

'They're a bit of a mystery,' I said, and all three of them leaned back, and I felt their attention return to disinterest.

'Door two,' said the central man. 'Straight through. Follow the signs.'

'Sorry, where?'

He jerked one thumb to the left. Yes, there were two doors, side by side, both white and plain. One bore a silver metal number one upon it, and the other bore a silver metal number two.

'Oh, right,' I said, 'Thank you.' I had no idea what I was thanking them for.

I did as I was told. Again.

Door number two opened to the street.

There was light rain. Telezon was noisy around me. I blinked at the backs of the buildings rising high, and the loitering people.

381

A QUEUE SYSTEM had been put in place that led down the side of the building and around the corner. A set of brass stands and yellow ropes marked the path, and I realised the people around me weren't loitering at all. They were part of the queue. Everyone wore a backpack.

The man boy human I'd met in the waiting room was directly ahead of me. He turned and nodded, as if we were all involved in a task that related to standing in the right place. There was no strangeness between us; it was as if events had made us friendly. 'How did that go?' he said, jerking his head back towards the door.

'I don't know. They asked some questions.'

'I'm not playing their game either,' he said, leaning forward, lowering his voice.

'What game?'

'The cha thing. I've got my own brain. I can see it for what it is.'

'What's that?'

He said the words very quietly, but with great intent. 'It's not real, is it? It's a manufactured distraction.' Then he turned back to face the queue as it shuffled forward, and I shuffled along with him.

The queue moved quite quickly.

Occasionally I looked behind me, as someone else emerged from the door. The old woman followed soon after me. There were others, mainly young, but not always. And I looked around the tall, dependable buildings that surrounded me and I felt real, solid, in the way that only administrative duties such as queuing can make a person feel.[69] Everything that had happened

---

69 There are so many historical sites of interest on this earth, and when you get there you mainly need to be patient and queue to get in. They are old, and get overwhelmed quickly. (Like me! Hah.) So we – the crew – decided against those sort of experiences early on, and after that we made a group pact not to care about old stuff so much. I think, in retrospect, it was a reflection of the

before was no longer quite me. Or, at least, it was a me that had been and gone. Those experiences had created this new me: the kind that stood in line for the hope of completion. Hadn't I been promised completion? Wasn't that just around the next corner?

If I couldn't have an answer, I was determined to have completion.

We moved forward, forward again. I turned the corner and found another line of queue ahead. The old woman behind me groaned when she saw it, loudly, and I felt both annoyed and sympathetic. Old groaner. The Spire was visible from this new angle, and I tilted back my head to enjoy the sight of it. The sky was very blue.

381

IN THE TIME that passed I became so real, so heavy, that I could barely lift my feet. I was exhausted; it came to me like a revelation. I was spent, and tired, and nothing was harder than that last line of questers, all of whom must have been tired too, tired to their cores. I kept hoping a rocket would leave, spurt up into new, clean space and somehow give me energy with the sight of it, but it

---

banning of longevity tech. Seventy years is not a long time to be alive. We all felt it – the need to live, in the moment, to the full.

I'm so glad we did, because of what happened next.

didn't. I kept watching, and then nobody was in front of me anymore and I was at the front of the queue.

I had been expecting a person. Maybe a person in a cha head, in that way people seemed to like to dress nowadays, but this was not a person at all. It was a robot. It had a square metal head and a rectangular metal body that encased a central screen. There were no arms or legs, but it had been given a face with round eyes and a slot of a mouth.

A message flashed up on the pink screen.

QUESTER

it read,

THANK YOU FOR TAKING PART
YOU ARE A HERO
PLEASE ACCEPT THIS TOKEN OF
APPRECIATION

A stiff piece of paper protruded from the slot beneath the eyes. I put my hand on it, and it came free.

GOODBYE

read the glass.

Aware of the people behind me, the pressure to move

on, I stepped away from the robot and walked down the street. It joined to a large road, more of an avenue really, that I remembered. People sauntered down it in fashionable outfits, although I spotted nobody in a cha head, which was both relieving and disturbing.

I knew the way from this avenue to the Spire, and that's where I ended up going, as if there had never been any other choice. I couldn't remember: had I always felt that this would be an important place to me? There at both the beginning and the end?

Standing before the Spire, it was as if nothing had changed. I watched people enter the building. Would they be on their way to the stars in a matter of hours? Off to conquer new places, new spaces. Perhaps they were the real heroes. What an adventure.

381

I LOOKED AT the piece of paper in my hand.

It read:

> *THIS TICKET ADMITS THE BEARER TO*
> *TELEZON SPIRE*
> *FOR ONE OUTWARD JOURNEY UPON THE*
> *ROCKET OF CHOICE*
> *VALID WITHIN 24 HOURS OF ISSUE ONLY*
> *PRESENT TO SPIRE INFORMATION DESK*

This.

This was what the First to Fall had wanted so badly. This was the dream. I had been given a way into a future without boundaries. The only question was—had I become brave enough to take it?[70]

I had twenty-four hours to make up my mind.

Well, twenty-three and a half hours.

---

70 For a long time I really did think this: we have a right to suffer. I mistook suffering for experience. I fully accept that my definition of suffering might be different to Fairly's definition, or anybody else's. How do you know?

Then there came a time – far out to sea, exploring the small islands of the south-eastern sectors – when our weather calmer stopped working and a localised storm blew up. We called to the spire, asked for help, but nobody corporeal was nearby and the weather calmer couldn't be fixed, it just wasn't a talent any of us possessed. We had concentrated on other skills: painting, cooking, sports. We could look up the plans of the device, but that did not mean we could translate that into manual action. We were, looking back at it, completely unprepared. We had enough information between us, in our young and confident bodies, to think we knew it all. We didn't. The *Commitment to Frivolity* capsized. We were in the water for forty-five minutes until another vessel managed to reach us. Forty-five minutes doesn't sound like a long time, does it? Particularly not to the parts of us that last for centuries. It was long enough for four members of the crew to drown, including my yellow-hatted captain.

Lost in thought, my feet took me back along familiar routes, past the park and the doctor's surgery, and the places where I had been a young, confused quester. So much had changed since then. I suppose I was looking for something to anchor me, for I glanced up and discovered I was on the path to return to the chime I had found while wandering around the city, despondent, feeling alone.

Once I reached it, I knew I had to try. I entered the booth, picked up the receiver, and said, 'Hello?' I honestly didn't expect it to work, not for me, a non-quester. I suspected somehow the chime would know the difference. But there she was: my mother.

'Hello,' she said, 'hello. Can I help? How are you doing?'

'Mum, it's me!' I said, 'It's me! I've finished! I'm back where I started, pretty much.'

She said, with a warmth in her voice that made me cry, 'Have you reached the end of the road, dear?'

'I think so. It went around in a big circle. Sort of.'

And then she said:

Sometimes the start and the end are the same place, and the only difference is the way you are facing.

She said:

Journeys only exist if you move to make them.

She said:

A circle looks exactly like a line if you see it from above.

I said, 'What does that even mean? They gave me a ticket into space! Do you think I should go into space?'

'You should go to where you need to be,' she said, 'I must ring off, I'm so sorry, I have another call waiting. Goodbye, dear. Good luck. Be brave.'

And the chime went dead.[71]

381

I STOOD IN the booth. The disquieting feeling grew that my mother had not even realised that she was speaking to me, her daughter, rather than to some random quester.

---

71 I was lucky enough to be abovedeck when the boat capsized. I survived by clinging to the hull. Trapped inside were my captain and three of my crewmates. They had a small pocket of air. I tried to make a hole, but the boat was so sturdily made! Of course it was. Centuries of human ingenuity augmented with stream information creates objects that cannot easily be destroyed. Who would think a situation would arise when you want to break something designed to last?

We tapped to each other through the hull. The sound reverberated. It was deep, so loud. I still hear those taps sometimes, when I wake at night. I no longer dream of losing numbers, but of losing people. Time passed so slowly. We tapped in a makeshift, easy code. One knock for 'A', two for 'B', and so on. I think I made out some words. I think one of them was love.

Then the tapping stopped.

I thought back through our previous conversations. Had she ever known she was speaking to me?

I made my way back to a familiar place: Old Joe's.[72] The bar where I had lived, and worked, and felt the first beginnings of happiness, I think, although I didn't know it at the time.

The place had been updated with neon and silver tubular stools, but I could see the same old bar underneath it all—Sam stood behind the counter, chatting to the few customers who occupied that blank time between lunch and the evening rush. I gave him my best smile, but he didn't seem to recognise me at first. Then it came to him—I saw the exact moment—and he said my name. He looked genuinely pleased to see me. He told me I could have a drink on the house.

This illusion of personal connection was enough for me. I took a seat on a tubular stool and he leaned in, delivering my tall glass of white wine. I told him of my adventures, and my ticket to space. He whistled. 'That's a hell of a prize,' he said.

'I could go home instead,' I said.

'They'd be glad to see you, I'm sure.'

I thought of the village. The farming and baking and the small schoolhouse, and the severe way of living,

---

72 Making a decision to return to familiar places is not easy. Particularly when those places contain memories of who you once were, and not who you are now.

without cars, without rockets to watch in the sky. The question was not whether they'd be pleased, but how long I could bear to stay there. I could never slot back into that tiny gap from which I'd emerged.

'I don't think I'm meant to go back,' I said.

'To the stars, then!' said Sam, and it sounded like the end of that strand of the conversation. He went back to serving, and I thought about the way other questers must have returned to the village and found a way to become part of that life again. Had their experiences been so different from mine? Had my mother's quest been nothing like my own? How, then, could she claim the knowledge to be a speaker?

381

IT'S STRANGE HOW we look for the past in every place we go.[73] We find it in familiar shapes and evocative feelings. We see it in smiles. Sam said there was nobody in the top room and he could do with extra staff that night, so I climbed back into my old role as a server and spent

---

73 Humans and their ability to hold so many ideas in their heads. For me, I have to admit that even though I knew our bodily lifespans were finite, I felt as though life onboard the *Commitment to Frivolity* would continue in the same vein forever. How could I think one thing and feel another? If I find a document that explains it in the two months left to me, I'll put a link in here.

the evening giving people one drink after another. Then I slept in a room in which I thought I felt the ghost of myself, watching with disappointment to find me there, even though every stick of furniture had been replaced and the walls painted over.

The sound of the drunkards spilling out on to the street and singing their way home: that was my memory, and my safe place for that night. I used it to latch on to the way I had felt when I first came to Telezon, keen and nervous, and younger. Yes, I had been younger.

I lay in the new bed and held my ticket in my hands.

The people who came to the bar and drank all night, every night, seemed certain there was no kind of tomorrow that would not look exactly the same as today.

I didn't know what *tomorrow* meant any more.

I lay awake, listening to the streets ebb and flow with the shufflers in the dark, and by dawn I had made my decision. No more tomorrows. No more sunrises. A rocket would leave in the morning, and I would be on it if I could.

Goodbye, old me. Hello, new me.

That was the decision I made.

Once the streets were daytime busy once more, I carefully repacked my backpack and went down to the bar, where Sam was already at work, bent over a row of figures in his ledger. 'You know,' he said, 'I think we always do better with a quester behind the bar. It's a draw. You could stay for a while longer if you liked.'

'I'm not a quester anymore,' I told him.

He nodded. 'You going up, then?'

'Up.'

'Out of this world,' he said, then, 'Go get 'em, tiger.'

I'd never been anybody's tiger before. It was a good feeling on which to end our friendship, for I would surely never see him again.

381

IT WAS, AS I remember it, all very easy.

I arrived at the information desk and showed the woman my ticket. She told me I could take the 10.43 to Completion 8.

I didn't know what Completion 8 was, but once it was explained to me by the assistant, using short, fast words, I was happy to accept. Apparently the Completions were worlds into which vast resources had already been sunk, transforming toxic atmospheres, building great towns and parklands, creating perfect places to start again. The assistant gave me a brochure and I looked at the pictures as I sat in the outgoing hall.

By that point, I had spent time in other waiting areas. Waiting had somehow turned into a big part of my life. This outgoing hall was a good waiting area; it offered free snacks and drinks, and there were slippery, glossy magazines on low tables next to comfortable armchairs. But it was still a space in which dormancy was the goal. I felt its torpor take me down, leave me numb, right at the point where I wanted to think, to feel, to experience.

Other people began to trickle in.

All of them were wearing backpacks too.

How quietly we sat, and had no thoughts at all.

Then the time finally came and we all boarded the rocket, and made what turned out to be only the first stop of the journey to Completion 8.

It was a blur. There were straps over my body, holding me in place in a padded seat: I remember that. The sensation of force, great force, and a feeling of exhilaration, of escape: now is the time, now, now, now. I was freed from so many things. Expectations of what I might become and what I might achieve, for instance. I left that behind and my mind felt wider, higher, more open as I closed my eyes and listened to the uplifting music provided through the complimentary headphones that plugged into the side of the seat. Many voices sang as one, a chorus of yearning, stirring, finding and keeping delight. I soared along with it.

Then, of course, that moment ended, as they all do, and the acceleration faded and I found I needed to pee, and a few people coughed.

381

THE MUSIC FADED and a voice informed me that we would dock with VoyCom 650 in ten minutes' time. I didn't know what that meant, but luckily the voice went on to explain in advertisement-speak:

> *VoyCom 650 is one of our state-of-the-art*
> *cruisers designed to take you in comfort and*
> *ease to the Completion planet of your choosing.*
> *During the fifty-three-year trip you will be*
> *retrained from quester to a profession that suits*
> *your carefully compiled personality profile;*
> *look forward to taking our fun, easy quizzes*
> *while on board, to work out your strengths and*
> *weaknesses! The VoyCom 650 also offers leisure*
> *and entertainment equipment at the cutting*
> *edge of technology, and offers a 99.2 per cent*
> *deep space survival rate. Thank you for choosing*
> *VoyCom!*

Fifty-three years.[74]

I fished the brochure out of my pocket and read it through again. Nothing about the length of time of the voyage had been mentioned. I sneaked glances at

---

74 That's a coincidence! That's exactly as long as I put this document down for.

the people sitting next to me, either side of my central position in the row, and none of them seemed surprised, or alarmed.

I had been an idiot not to realise it could hardly be a short trip. I should have thought it through. Fifty-three years, signed away, to be taken up with quizzes and personality tests.

This is what happens when a person doesn't pay attention. Mistakes are made.

If I had really looked at the offer, at what was being dangled in front of me, I would have realised, surely. Nobody else could be to blame for this turn of events. I started to sweat; I felt perspiration dripping from my armpits. I squirmed. I wanted no-one to smell me. The music returned, but the feeling of soaring inspiration was gone, and the voices grated. I realised I wasn't only dripping from my armpits. I was crying, and I couldn't stop, and the water was falling on my lap, and the only thing I had, to attempt to mop it up, was the brochure. The material was stiff, far from absorbent. The more I swiped at my face with it, the more hot and scratched and drippy I felt, and nobody looked at me, nobody asked if I was all right. Nobody cared at all. I had left everybody who cared behind.

381

I CAME ACROSS Cecile on around day thirty.[75]

I was in the cafeteria after a long artificial day of filling out questionnaires, early in the reassignment process, and there she was, in the queue ahead of me, trying to pick up a thin slice of pizza with plastic tongs. Eventually she gave up on the tongs and slid the slice out from the tray with her fingers, then took a guilty glance around

---

75 Once you start to look for coincidence, you see it everywhere. There was a time that we realised three of us in the crew had the same middle name, and it was really tempting to think that destiny had brought us together in some way, but that's not true. It's too obvious to turn coincidence into meaning. I'm not actively advocating against finding meaning, I should say. I just think that it doesn't have to be everything. Although I'm starting to wonder if returning to the beginning, retracing steps, telling stories about one's own life, isn't all part of the same pernicious instinct. Am I making sense? Then I must be doing it wrong.

Here's what's going to happen. In two months' time I'll upload my personality to the Unity Spire and live in the non-corporeal for a while. I can't say how long. Long enough to forget the taste of apples, and the sound of the sea. Then I'll sign up for another stint in a new body, get slotted into a baby, and become part of a new person, and a new set of experiences. Not as myself, but as a new me. I get to be a new me. I hope I remember some of these thoughts. Imagine going right back to the beginning.

the room as she turned to find a seat and—bam. She saw me. She recognised me straight away, as I had known her. We were still little girls, somehow, under all that had happened, and that was the most obvious thing about us.

She couldn't fight her way back through the queue to me, so I grabbed whatever foodstuff was close— mashed potato surprise—and hurried through the one-way system to her, and we sat at a small table in a sea of small tables, and expressed things with our eyes. I think my eyes were mainly mirroring hers when it came to relief and confusion. The overriding vibe on board VoyCom was that it wasn't cool to talk about the quest, or the past, or the planet we'd left behind, really. It was all geared towards the amazing future. But really I just wanted to say to Cecile: *what happened? Where did you go? How did you end up here?* And to also say: *I'm so glad I'm not alone.* But none of these things were really socially acceptable.

Still, we had a good meal together and then we went to the observation platform and looked out over the universe, the stars and the black and the lack of anything familiar except each other. That feeling was the strongest glue; it bound us together so tightly that we were inseparable, for a while, taking all our meals at the same little table and thinking that between us we were making a connection back to home, to the place where we'd both begun our heroic stories.

But the feeling began to fade, and Cecile made some new friends that I didn't really get on with, and soon it became painful to be around her and not to feel able to ask all those questions I wanted answered.

381

Fairly: It's so weird, isn't it? How far we've come?

Cecile: Yeah, it is so weird.

Fairly: From our tiny village, from dancing at the hall and birthday parties and your dad's boat—I mean—I know we're not supposed to—but I just mean—none of that really prepared us for life, did it? For what came next? Whatever that was, for you, I mean—I'm not asking, but there must have been experiences we had in common.

Cecile: We've got *this* experience in common. The refectory, the quizzes, the dorms. And loads to go. Have you tried the mashed potato surprise?

Fairly: Yeah, I have.

Cecile: What was the surprise?

Fairly: I don't think I worked that out.

Cecile: The surprise is that there's no surprise, huh.

Fairly: After the journeys we've had, yeah, I can see that coming as a surprise.

Cecile: Really?

Fairly: I just mean—not a lot of it made sense to me.

Cecile: Hopefully it made more sense than the mashed potato surprise.

Fairly: How have you been doing on the quizzes?

Cecile: Really well, I think. Yeah. Looking forward to getting the results, but I think I'll probably be up for something really cool. Like a pilot. I have excellent manual dexterity.

Fairly: Really? Didn't see much of that when we went boat rowing that time.

Cecile: Ha, no. Ha.

(Silence)

Fairly: You good with heights, are you? Did you find that out with the trip in the hot air balloon? Because I was terrified the whole time. I mean, I think it's probably okay to talk about that bit because it was the end of the quest, wasn't it?

Cecile: A hot air balloon?

Fairly: Yeah.

Cecile: Cool.

(Silence)

Cecile: I might go down the gym for a bit. I've just realised—that's really weird, isn't it? I said, 'go down the gym,' but the gym is up and along, isn't it? It's up from here. The elevators keep confusing me, all the buttons in a long horizontal row so you never know whether you're going up or down, but I met this girl in the gym and she said we were really high up. Or did she mean in space? Can you be high up in space?

Fairly: I don't know.

381

CECILE AND I stopped hanging out so much.[76] She had her new friends, and I had my thoughts, which were getting more and more complex with every artificial day.

The first round of quizzes completed, I had been assigned to the egg-watching apprentice programme. It

---

76 It's terribly hard, to come to the end of a relationship. I always knew it would happen. Perfection doesn't last, right?

After the death of my beautiful yellow-hatted captain I got a message on my thoughtboard to ask if I wanted to return and head up the Department of Lived Experience at higher socialisation since I had amassed so much relevant knowledge.

I turned it down. I thought at the time that I couldn't face claiming to know what those deaths, that loss, meant. But now I think I was attempting to run away from that inevitable process.

involved watching for the exact moment when giant blue eggs hatched, and recording the time. Artificial eggs were being used for training purposes, so I wasn't certain if I would actually be expected to monitor giant blue eggs once I reached Completion 8, or if they would be smaller eggs—or, indeed, what would emerge from such eggs. Obviously, nothing ever emerged from the artificial eggs. I tried to pay attention, but I hated the job immediately, and had already applied to take the questionnaires again.

How could they have missed all the good things about me? I thought during my confident moments.

They've worked out I'm useless, I thought, in times of doubt.

Not having a quest was taking some time to adjust to. Others were managing much better than I was. How happy they looked, as if the rocket was where they were always meant to be. But what would that mean once they reached Completion 8? Surely *that* was the end point?

I don't know why I was so obsessed with end points. I think I was still imagining that every story had one.

And then, on artificial day 81, I saw him.

The breathing man.

He was on the other side of the glass in the egg chamber, in the supervisory booth. He was smiling. He looked pleased to see me, or maybe pleased with himself.

A thousand thoughts flashed through my mind, from the first time I'd heard him, lying on the other side of the wall not far from my village. I had been so close to home; why hadn't I just turned back? Said that this life wasn't for me? I could have turned back. And the other times I had seen him. The time he had kidnapped me, run away with me, sailed with me, stood with me in his pavilion.

I remembered how it felt to be so close to him that I felt he could have crawled inside me and stopped my heart with his hands.

381

THE MAN IN the kiosk had told me there would be no more visits from the breathing man.[77]

I had believed him. I had taken his word for it. I was an idiot. I remained an idiot, trusting people, swallowing their statements. Forty-three years on board to go, in the company of the breathing man. And then a new planet with him, looking for me, joined to me. Every move I made would only demand a countermove from him.

I would never be without him.

———————

77 There's no escaping certain things without losing yourself entirely. I tried for so long to escape I swore I would never get on a boat again. I took to the land, and I walked. I followed roads. I think, maybe, on some level, I was looking for a Horned Road.

But I had to try.

I left the training room, abandoned the eggs. I ran down the corridors of the training department, moving so fast I thought I would break free, snap out of the feelings he made me feel. I hit the sixth reception area at speed, and the people lounging there, enjoying table tennis or browsing the free bookshelves, stared at me, with shock in their features, as I sprinted past. They were all young, like me. They were heroes like me, and not one of them could have helped me. I saw it in their expressions. Was it against the rules to run? I'd been given a bulky guide to etiquette upon arrival onboard. But no, I didn't care, I refused to care. There were always rules, so many rules. All us ex-questers had been spoon-fed on rules from the beginning.

I think I was trying to run right through the ship and out the other side. I didn't look behind me. There was no point. He was always there. At some point I would turn and see him. I ran through one of the themed cafes, through the manufactured arboretum, and into living quarters T-Z. The sections passed and my lungs burned and my legs were lead, but I did not stop until there was no more room to run. The deck narrowed to a cylindrical staircase—up or down? I chose up. I began to ascend.

Stairs. Exhausting. Still, upwards, curving and the case narrowing until I reached a door. Upon it was a small brass sign, highly polished, that read:

1. OBSERVATION AND TELEMETRY[78]

I honestly didn't think it would open, but it did. It opened for me. Doors are made for opening, just as heroes are made for obedience.

381

I ENTERED A dark space, shadowed, pillars regularly spaced through the chamber—a holy sort of atmosphere, like a grand church. High above me was a transparent ceiling rising to a steeple, with only the depths of space beyond it. Low-level lighting was set in the floor: glowing yellow bulbs. Unblinking eyes.

A lone light rose from the floor on a central pillar, and milling around it were cha. A *lot* of cha. Large cha— human-sized. Were they humans in costumes? If they were, the outfits were incredibly lifelike. I couldn't tell.

---

78 Where are we all going? I hate the need for the question, but I understand it a whole lot better now. I have a theory about this:

We're going to the place that makes sense of where we've been.

That's why I'm annotating this document once more. To prove that. Here's total honesty: I do want it to mean something. I want to be remembered for being a collection of experiences that can be communicated to others. Isn't that terrible? Is that what being alive is all about?

Their heads swivelled as one in my direction.

I had not moved from the doorway. It occurred to me that maybe they could not see me properly; maybe I was only a silhouette, framed, my features hidden. I tried to keep my breaths even, my fears controlled.

'Get. Out.'

It was a human voice. Wasn't it? One of them had said it. I had no idea which one. I backed out, let the door swing shut. There were no more stairs to climb. I had to go back the way I had come.

Downstairs is easier than upstairs, at least, on the body, but on the mind—well, retracing worn steps can be deadly. I've never felt so vulnerable before or since as I did on that retreat. The breathing man: where was he? I tried to see past the line of the steps. I listened for footsteps. I moved stealthily, warily. No more running for me.

But at least it's easier to see things that have previously been missed when sprinting in panic, and there, jutting off from the staircase, was a short hallway that led to another door.

4. CONTINGENCY

That sounded like my kind of deck.

The door opened and admitted me to a cold, unused, ovoid space. It reminded me of the large eggs I had been given to watch. And many smaller eggs jutted off, more ovals, sealed by snug hatches with portholes in their centre. I approached one, and peered inside. There was a bed, a chair, some boxes. A white desk with a screen upon it that was, perhaps, a control panel. I checked the next porthole and found exactly the same layout within. I found them sinister. Threatening, in their homogeneity.

381

I WALKED ON, looking through each porthole, until I came to an alcove of shelves, each one holding cha heads to be worn, and soft cha fur costumes folded up in the slots beneath. I stroked one. It took me back to the farm, to the mountain chalet; it felt so realistic I was certain it had been stitched together from real cha skin, if that was a thing.

Did that mean the creatures on Deck One were definitely humans in costume, then? I still couldn't say for sure. The eyes had looked at me like real cha eyes. But the voice—hadn't that, undoubtedly, been human? I had no way to make sense of it for the next forty-three years at the very least, during which time I would have to retrain in some terrible job and see the breathing man around every corner. I couldn't bear it, even if a paradise world waited for me at the end of it.

The cha heads were horrible. Lifeless. The noses were shiny and cold, and the triangular ears were stubby and hard. Wait. I ran my fingers back over the small protuberances. They weren't ears. Horns. The cha had tiny triangular horns—all this time, and I had never understood.

They were horned creatures found on a horned road.[79]

There was some deep meaning here, deep as space, as sea, and I could not understand it, not while I was part of it. And there would never be a way to get free and view it dispassionately. Even arriving on another planet would not allow me to escape.

I heard footsteps.

Footsteps, close.

I could see nothing. I stared around the room. Nothing.

Footsteps.

I put my hand to the hatch of the nearest chamber, and it let out a hiss and swung back. I dived inside, slammed the hatch shut. A chair, desk, bed. No place to hide. Next to the hatch was a red cord, and a sign in red:

In Case of Emergency

---

79 I never did find my own Horned Road. Every path led to a new choice, a new adventure, but I never saw a signpost that offered to give me meaning.

I pulled it, hard, said: *please?* There was a grating sound, so loud my ears burned, then the pod flipped over, spun, and came free with a shudder from VoyCom 650. I was free from the rocket. I was heading out into deepest, unknown space.[80]

381

How fast VoyCom 650 became a dot.

I lay on the bed and watched through the porthole. I didn't much care where I was going as long as I was escaping, at that point. The word 'home' popped

---

80 I can't claim to have ever gone to outer space, but I did request the shutdown of my link to the Unity Spire for a few years. If that isn't bravery in this Age of Curation (who is being curated? how?), then I don't know what is. Without that link there were no updates, no thoughtboard, no care packages. But there was loneliness.

When I couldn't bear it anymore, I found a community of like-minded people, but a community of people who want to be alone is a weird concept, and we all felt the strain. At least, I think we did. I found them in a cave, high up in the south-south-east mountains, at the gateway to the Negatory Tract that had offered me a place. At that point I was seriously considering it.

The people gathered there to make their decision – would they let the streamed side of their existence die along with their body, when the time came? Would they cease to exist entirely?

into my thoughts. I wanted to assume that the pod's direction had my best interests at heart, although that seemed ridiculous, to continue to hold some theory of beneficence in the universe. How naïve I still was.

Once there was no sign of the ship anymore, I got up and poked around.

The pod was larger than it had seemed from the outside, and it was not, in fact, an ovoid. One of the curved side panels slid back, revealing two delineated areas: the first, a small wash area and toilet; the second, crates, stacked three abreast, topped with a bulky cha costume and head. I eyed it warily. It would not make for pleasant company, but there was nowhere else to put it, except—should I risk trying to stuff it into the toilet? What if it blocked? I had no idea how long the pod would have to house me.

'Better not risk it,' I said to myself, already thinking my own voice would be better company than none, and at that moment, right at that second of acceptance that I really was on my own, the cha costume unfolded and the head lifted, and I was not alone at all. A cha. A man, the human hands lifting to the head, the head being twisted free, him underneath it, with his hair tousled and his eyes so quick to find mine, the breathing man.

He was right there, he was so close, he had me now. No way to run. He had finally cornered me in a place without corners, an escape pod without escape. I wanted to scream at him: *get out, get out*, but I didn't dare to open my mouth, not for what might come out, or what he might reach over and put in. He was so close. I thought he would touch me, be on me, then inside me, there was only the thinnest of barriers between us, and whatever I was, whatever personality I possessed, would be hollowed out and filled only with him.

381

His mouth opened and closed.

He formed words. Whatever he was saying, I couldn't hear. Was he making sounds? Why couldn't I hear them? He pointed at me. Not at me, but behind me. The desk. I didn't dare to turn around. He looked so much older since the last time I'd looked at him properly. He was tired, or ill. I thought I must also look that way to him, and that realisation forced me to risk speaking.

'What?' I said.

He pointed again, and took a step forward. His lined, weathered face showed frustration; I could feel the emotion pouring from him. I had such thoughts whenever he was close; such sad, strange thoughts. I moved back as he approached, keeping the same distance between us. He stopped at the desk, pointed to it again. There was a notepad and a pen, some small stationery items. 'Write it down?' I asked. A firm shake of the head. More pointing, to one particular item on the desk.

It was a miniature chain device.

I thought I had seen the last of those, but it was undoubtedly a chain device—a sleek silver box with a red button on top.

I had thought my quest was over.

I was told as much.

Was this part of the quest?

Did the quest go on forever?

I might be pressing buttons forever, finding these devices and repeating these same actions, and he would be there: the breathing man. We would continue to play our roles, as if we had absolutely nothing better to do.

'Why?' I asked him.

His eyes slid from my face to the device, then back to my face.

'Where did you come from? Is this your job? Can you not just... go away?' What a stupid question, in the middle of space. Of course he could not just go away.

Seconds passed.

If he had wanted to hurt me, he would have done it already. It was not possible to keep panicking, to maintain pumping adrenaline through my system, when nothing was happening. My head began to clear. I thought through options. I had no options, so that was easy.

I had to find a way to be in this pod with him.

'If you hurt me...' I said.

381

IF HE HURT me, I would be in pain. I might die. I might hurt him back. Whatever I had been running from, it was to happen right here, right now.

'Bring it on,' I said.

I came to him, so slowly. He did not so much as shift his weight. When I was beside him, I put my hand on the tiny button of the miniature chain device.

I pushed the button, and at first it seemed that—

We will be stuck together for years.[81] We will be in this

---

81 I didn't last long in those mountains. It became clear to me very quickly that I like order. I also like the illusion of disorder. Why do I want both? Anyway, while I was there I fended for myself, and ate what I could get, and didn't order my thoughts in the least, and I think that's why it's really hard for me to remember exactly what happened there.

I have a few memories.

I learned to dance. Yes. There was an instructor living in those mountains; she had once been a magnificent dance champion, and she had left it all behind to offer lessons to anyone who came along. She looked starved and proud. I mean: who wants dance lessons up there? You'd need a level of self-belief that rivals the highest peaks to keep

pod, hands joined, with nothing to do for years, and we will grow older and we will get to know each other so well, intimately, and it will start the moment I take my hand from this button, and I'll notice how the pod seems larger, quieter, safer. I'll look around in surprise and he will say something I can hear, for the first time. His voice will be pleasant. Whatever he says will be enough to make me re-evaluate him, and the things that have happened between us. That does not mean I will instantly forgive him. I certainly won't automatically trust him, for that ship has sailed forevermore and I won't quite trust anybody ever again, but I will rethink him.

I will find, within me, space for him.

I will stop fighting him.

I will accept that escaping him was never an option, and I will see how every attempt to wriggle free brought us to

---

going with that choice. But I took a lesson or two, because I wanted someone to touch my body. I was starving for it. She held me very firmly. I remember that. She taught me a strange, old dance. One-two-three, one-two-three. I asked her why she had given up doing something she was so good at, and she said: *I hated having to follow the same old steps.* Then she showed me a dance she had made up, herself, from scratch. It was… really odd. I didn't get it at all. It didn't even look much like a dance. *Of course*, she said, *it owes a lot to everything else. There's no escaping it all, really, is there?*

this point. I will be uncomfortable with that knowledge for a long time, even while we go on completing such mundane tasks as using the toilet and taking it in turns to sleep. It will hurt me, but I will realise this pain has never been avoidable. We will sort out supplies from the crates, and we will have long conversations, hearing the sound of his pleasant voice in the deep cold of space, and I will tell him everything in return, and he will be a good listener.

But I don't think, even after years together, years in which we have revealed everything and found neither of us knows any more than the other, that I will be able to forgive him for having to be part of my life.[82]

---

82 We need people. We have to have people. We hate people. We hate emotions. We hate ourselves. We're young and free and old and troubled and alone and part of something and everything all at once. There was a time when I saw a girl who looked just like me. She was drinking in a bar, not unlike Old Joe's: a small place with an atmosphere that warmed up in the evenings. I sat and watched her. She was waiting for someone who did not come. I wanted nothing more than to go to her and say, 'I'm here, I see you. I am you.' That's how I feel about Fairly. I am her. All the events of my life have been influenced by her. I can't escape her steps on her road. We're the same and yet she is still a mystery to me.

EVERY TIME I ask him why he followed me he will only shake his head, and I will ask him often. It's the question for which he has no answer. I will remember why I must never, never, quite trust him. Not completely, not utterly. It would be wrong to trust him. He is not free to be my friend. He will forever be, somehow, my enemy, even when we reach the point when I can predict every move he will make. If only he could answer that one question.

This is his life.

It will always be his life.

I will always think of 'always' as a difficult word. Feelings will change, life will change, every moment. There will come a time when we are no longer in space. Possibly even a time when the Earth fills the porthole, a perfect blue circle, and then we see continents—brown—and clouds—white. The green, a most delicate set of shades, and I will look at them tenderly. He will say something meaningful about the reason for the journey. About how we are part of each other, have shared so much, learned beyond knowledge, but still he will not answer the question: why? I will cry a little at his magnificent speech and we will hug, and I'll say something profound too. It will not be enough to take us away from who we are, and when the pod lands, the worst is over, and the hatch swings open to admit the blue, my first thought will be:

When can I get away from you?

He will know it. He will take my hand and squeeze it, and ask for my forgiveness, because we both already know that as soon as I take a step in any direction he'll be behind me.

So I won't take a step.

I'll stay in the pod, and return to the miniature chain device, and I will put my hand on the button. He will nod, and put his hand over mine, and we will press the button one more time, and at first it seemed that nothing had happened at all, but then Fairly's eyes returned to the world outside the hatch. Home. She was home. There was strength to be found in that.

381

IT WAS A new chapter. She did not have to be the person her experiences had made her.

The breathing man took his hand from hers. She saw his realisation of her rejection of him in his eyes. He had to follow, and she had to say it.

'Get out. Get out!'

He shook his head.

No matter who she became next, there he would be.

'All right, then,' she said. 'If that's the way it has to be. Come on. Let's go.'

She collected her backpack and led the way to the hatch,

out into the afternoon sun. The sea, calm and bright, was on her left, beyond a deserted stony beach. On her right was a long stretch of road. It looked familiar.

The breathing man coughed discreetly behind her. He had collected the cha costume and head, tucked under his arm. Fairly said, 'You want those, huh? Are you going to wear them?' He shrugged. 'I'm pretty certain,' she said, 'It's this way.' She had no idea how she knew; built-in programming, on some level. 'Yep. Home's this way.'

What did she mean by *home*? The village, of course. She was ready to see it again. To settle. She put her feet on the road and felt certain it was the horned road. Once upon a time it had called to her, urged her to move her feet forward. Now it beckoned her to return.

'Keep up,' she said, over her shoulder.

She started walking. She felt the familiar weight of the backpack as a comfort rather than an obligation. How strange it was to have come full circle, so far, no distance at all. The breathing man did not try to keep her company, journey with her. He preferred to lurk, way back in the roadside bushes, or behind rocks, or just beyond the previous bend. She would occasionally catch a glimpse of him, and be both irritated and comforted by the feelings he aroused in her. Here she was, different yet the same, and the world was friendly to her footsteps right now. Who knew how long that state of affairs would last?

Yes, there were lessons she had learned well. She

wanted to take them back to her village, and find out what happened next.

381

TWO NIGHTS OF camping, and on the third night Fairly found herself at the boundary wall at dusk. She lay down in her sleeping bag, not bothering to erect the tent. She knew the breathing man would lie on the other side of the wall. She waited in an ecstasy of expectation for him, as dusk turned to night. Eventually he came, and she heard his soft sighs, so close. She put a hand to the wall, where she imagined he lay. Had there ever been a time without him? Once, when she was very young, without a quest. She had been a little girl, but even then she wondered if he hadn't been lurking on the other side of her bedroom wall. Or had he trained her to think of him as eternal, indispensable? She only knew she could no longer be a person without him. What a terrible thought that was. She couldn't sleep for it.

As soon as the sun arrived, peeping over the hills, Fairly got up, packed her things, and set off as silently as she could. Let him sleep, she thought, and refused to check behind her as she hurried away. She made it to the gates of her village in three days, and stood outside for a while, waiting, undecided if the moment had properly come for her to return to the beginning.

'Fairly?'

It was not someone she knew well. But it was someone she knew: the baker. Someone who had just happened to be passing the gate, and now they looked upon her as if she was something special. A hero, maybe. A story, returning for a proper ending.

A burial: that was the thought that flashed through Fairly's mind, and she pushed it away.

'I'm still alive,' she said, out loud, surprising herself, and the baker—Mrs Taft, that was the name—said, 'Well of course, we never thought otherwise, come in, come in, your mother will be so pleased!' And she was swept up in the baker's enthusiasm, which she half-remembered along with big forearms and a liking for fizzy wine. And the cake![83] Of course. The cake from

---

83 The first thing I did when I returned to the Jurassic coast was go and visit my mother. She had made a cake. It wasn't great (she never did become a wonderful cook, not for lack of trying) but I can't think of anything I've enjoyed more.

She died thirty years ago. During that time I spent time with her, walking and talking and laughing, and eventually I gave in, and took the job at the Department of Lived Experience. I helped lots of people make their own adventures, and I never once wanted any of them to suffer. If I have saved anybody from that, then I am glad, even if it means I robbed them of the chance to grow. Whatever growing is.

Fairly's leaving party, before she pressed the very first button. The cake had been fruit-laden, covered in a thick yellow icing. Delicious.

381

THE BAKER LED her to the village hall, back to the departure lounge, which was bare, the chairs and tables stacked away. 'If I'd known you were coming, I would have baked your favourite,' said Mrs Taft. 'Fruit cake! I remember. Stand right there. Don't move.'

Fairly did as she was told as Mrs Taft rushed off to fetch people. It was an odd sensation—to stand still. She didn't even take off her backpack, so completely did she want to preserve the feeling of being out of time, released from its obligations. Then her mother came in at a run, and hugged her tightly, in a wordless grip. Her mother looked older. 'I worried and worried,' said her mother. 'Why did you never use the chime? You could have called me on the chime.'

'I did!' Fairly said, but her words were lost as loud Mrs Taft said over and over, 'I found her! I found her!' as if credit needed to be taken, kept close. An impromptu party developed. A cake was found, not as fancy as the leaving cake, but still good, sweet. And there was wine when the mayor turned up, a bottle in each hand and a smile as wide as the sea. The wine was bubbly, and it made Fairly's mood rise and then fall until she felt nothing good at all, and wished she hadn't come back to all this fuss over nothing.

Cecile's parents arrived at the end, hanging back, looking wan. Fairly went to them, drawn by their lack of effort.

'I saw Cecile,' she said. 'She was doing well.'

Cecile's mother perked up a little. 'Maybe she'll come back soon, then,' she said.

'Maybe.' For there was nothing else she could say, and no way to explain the rocket, and her own decision to jump ship. It was easier to let them believe that the quest could end—wasn't she proof of that?

Fairly wandered over to the chain device in the corner, loosely covered with an old sheet. Everyone had started singing old songs. She doubted they remembered why the party had started in the first place.

She put one hand on the button, through the cloth. No. She wouldn't press it, not this time. Enough pressing and being pressed.

381

'YOU COMFY?' SAID her mother.

Fairly nodded. She was back in her own bed, feeling too large for the room and everything in it. Her mother had entered the room without knocking, and that, too, she felt too large for. She remembered the nights in the open and the years in the pod. Among other things.

'What an adventure!' her mother said. 'Will you tell it to me, some time?'

'Tell me yours,' Fairly suggested, and her mother said, 'No, no, no, you don't want to hear about all that. I never even lasted a week, just turned around and came back at the first hint of trouble.'

'Really?'

'Nearly everyone does. I mean—but your dad was gone for longer. And he told me, after you were born, that he hoped you were like him, and you lasted the course. He wanted you to be a real hero. Like him. That was why he had to go again.'

'He... walked the horned road again?'

Her mother nodded vaguely.

'So when did he die?'

'I couldn't give you a date, exactly. Some time after that.'

A suspicion came to Fairly. 'He died, though. Right? You said he died. He's not still out there walking the road?'

'Isn't it nearly the same thing?' her mother said.

'No!' said Fairly, who could see that it really was nearly the same thing to her mother. It was a revelation.

Her mother must have seen the shock on her face. 'Well, I'll leave you to get a good night's sleep,' she said, and left.

Fairly lay in bed.

She wondered where the breathing man was.

She wanted to say to him: *Dead is not the same as gone.*

She wanted to say: *Just walking down the road and coming back again is not the same as trying to find some answers.*

She thought the breathing man might listen to her. But when she held her own breath, she could tell nobody was in the room with her. And she couldn't stop breathing forever; she had to start again, in, out, in, out, in, out. The bedroom was so small—how much air could be inside it? There was not enough to fill her lungs properly, and it was already affecting her ability to keep living.

381

DID IT MATTER, though? Did it matter, as long as she was soft and warm and loved, and nobody made a big deal of anything? Did it matter if it only mattered to her?[84]

---

84 So many things have mattered to me. The boat, the crew. This document. My captain. Dancing and travelling and living. I've seen so much, met so many people. After my mother died, I left the Department of Lived Experience. I joined an archaeological party and spent years living on a boat once more, diving under the ocean, digging up the real relics of ages past – things you can touch, hold. Some of them have obvious meanings: cups, forks, cooking utensils. Things of the body. Others remains mysterious,

Her mother worked every day in the study, hovering over the chime, repeating the same soothing words. Fairly felt a renewed interest in those calls, knowing now that her mother was not offering guidance from the point of view of personal experience after all. What, then, motivated her mother's words? She took to hanging around in the study, listening in, feeling a prickle of her own opinions with each banal statement her mother uttered.

There was a steady stream of calls.

'You didn't recognise me,' Fairly said once, mildly, in between the desperate demands of the questers for advice. 'I phoned, and you didn't recognise me.'

'Doesn't every piece of wisdom sound a little bit alike, no matter who utters it, no matter why?' pondered her mother.

At one time this kind of statement would have satisfied Fairly; how incurious and accepting she had been. 'Who pays you?' she demanded. 'How did you get this job?'

'Somebody has to do it, and I was willing. And that is reward enough.'

---

and those are the ones I have cherished. I catalogued them all under the correct tag of Unknown Purpose (UNK99999999) and submitted them to the relevant museums. But for the ones that seemed so outlandish, so strange, that they defied all explanation, I created my own sneaky tag. You can look them up under FAI00009760. I call them Fairly Objects.

'So it doesn't make money? Or do they pay you in cha?'

'Who, exactly, is *they*?' Her mother frowned at her. Fairly felt she'd touched on a sore point. 'Listen,' her mother said. 'When things are beyond our understanding, it pays to learn to think beyond understanding things.'

'What does that even mean?'

'It means that sometimes less knowledge is better.'

It occurred to Fairly that her mother was only saying that because she had no actual knowledge.

But it only made her own thirst for answers stronger.

She spent longer and longer in the study, listening to the calls, trying to work out if there was any information contained within the statements her mother made. She could not be sated.

The accumulation of answers that gave no illumination reached a point of critical mass, a sort of weight so substantial that Fairly carried it, not unlike the old backpack that now sat on the shelf in her room next to her stuffed cha. It had achieved its own importance beyond meaning. It made her feel… wise.

381

SHE STOPPED ASKING questions between the calls on the chime.

She drowsed in the afternoon sunshine, disapproving

of everything her mother said, feeling clever for having spotted its uselessness.

At that point, her mother offered her a turn at the job of speaker.

'There's more than enough work for two,' she said.

'Say all the usual, is it?' She smiled. 'Call everyone *dear*, and tell them to abide?'

'You've got it!' said her mother. 'You'll be great.'

Fairly thought about it. She could easily picture a future where she and her mother formed a real, deep bond on the basis of sharing this role. Then her mother would become infirm, and she would take over the job on her own, and maybe make a child of her own to take over the job one day from her, and make up some stuff about a brave father or whatever. She would send the child off on their own quest and hope they would return, exactly as she had, exactly this level of repetition.

It was thinking about the future, feeling it as a vanishingly rare opportunity to control her own direction, that took Fairly back to the feeling in the escape pod, and she knew what she had to do before she could reply to her mother's offer.

'I'll be back shortly,' she said, and left the room.

She left the house.

She left the village.

She stood at the start of the horned road and called for him.

'Are you there?' she cried, out to the world beyond. 'Breathing man, are you still close?'[85]

When he came out from behind a rock, he was in costume.

He was proud in the cha head, moving with an awareness, a presence, that she had not seen in him before. But it was still him. Her breathing man. She knew him.

He didn't come close. He stayed a way down the road, and held out one hand. An invitation, to come to him. She didn't know if she wanted it or not; she waited to see what her feet would do. Once before they had brought her here. She would trust them to see if they would take her away again.

No.

No, she did not move.

She called out, 'Are you my father?'

381

HE MADE NO response to that.

---

85 I'll leave you to finish Fairly's journey in her words, with only her thoughts as your company. I owe her that much. I'll just say that I envy Fairly her ability to make friends with her breathing man, or at least, being able to tolerate him. I don't think I ever quite managed it myself. It's so difficult to forgive the breathing man for existing, even if everything did turn out all right in the end. Didn't it?

'You're not, are you?' she said.

The breathing man shuffled his feet. He looked a little uncomfortable with that line of questioning.

So she said, 'Why are you dressed like that?'

He tilted his head, as if the question was strange, unfathomable. The doubt shot through her—*Is this my breathing man at all?* But she had been sure, only a moment ago. Was there never any certainty, ever? Was nothing to be trusted?

'I'm Fairly,' she said. 'You know me. Fairly.' She realised she had never told him her name before.

He dropped his hand.

Then, from all around, from the woods and the rocks, in every direction, they came. Men in costumes, wearing the fluffy bodies, the tiny horns of the cha. They came to the breathing man, forming a line—no, a circle, that wrapped around the village. They surrounded her. They stood in silence.

A high, loud sound came from behind her. A scream. Then her mother was there, standing at her elbow. 'What have you done?' she said, her eyes round, her lips white and trembling.

'They just showed up,' said Fairly.

'They're never invited in. We send you out to them. That's why we send you out.'

This was too much to make sense of. 'I didn't invite anyone in.'

'You're talking to them!'

'Cha!' screamed someone, from inside the village. A cry went up. 'Cha! Cha!'

'Send them away,' begged her mother.

'They're not real cha,' said Fairly, trying to keep her voice on the side of reasonable. She could hear many other voices behind her now; the villagers were assembling. A pressure was growing. She was caught in the centre of it. It was crushing her. She tried again, finding her voice hoarse. 'Look. They're only people wearing costumes. Not real cha, and cha wouldn't hurt you anyway. They're only standing there.'

The mayor appeared. His wide smile was gone: his eyes were narrowed, his chin jutting forwards. Underneath that jolly exterior had been a menacing presence, all along. 'Tell them to get out!'

'But I...'

'I protect this village,' he said, low, in her ear. 'That's the job that was given to me. It's up to you to prove that you want to protect it too.'

381

'LOOK,' SHE SAID, determined to try to be honest. 'The one in the middle is my breathing man. From my quest. He's taken to wearing the outfit, that's all. So I could tell him to take the outfit off, but I've already come to terms with the fact that I can't make him get out and stay out. The world doesn't work that way.'

'You've been talking to them,' said the mayor in a shocked tone, and the other villagers made disapproving sounds.

'I thought you understood,' said her mother. 'We send the children out so *they* don't come in.'

'They're not what you think they are!' Fairly called out to her breathing man, 'Please, could you just take off the head, just for a minute? You'd be doing me a huge favour.'

The breathing man lifted up his arms and grasped the cha head. He pulled it free. The others followed suit.

They were all the same.

They were all her breathing man.

Identical in every aspect of their faces: breathing men. No difference. Too identical to even be siblings. There was no way to tell one from another, to get to know one as an individual. Seeing them en masse made Fairly want to run away, as far and as fast as she could.

But she knew that feeling, and she knew she didn't want to play that game anymore. She couldn't possibly win it.

There was only one course of action.

'Right,' she said. 'Everyone come on in.'

'No!' cried the villagers. 'No!'

But it was too late. All the breathing men piled in, fast, as the villagers scattered, and screamed, and fled.

One breathing man came to stand close to her, so close she could smell him. He smelled of sweat: fresh, energising.

'It's you, isn't it?' she said.

He mouthed words, but no sound came out.

'What next?' she asked him.

He looked at her as if to say—*Shouldn't you know? Aren't we playing by your rules, now?*

Am I in charge? she wondered.

If she was, she supposed she ought to act like it.

She marched back into the village, and started the difficult business of trying to get people to understand something she didn't understand herself. Was that what being a grown-up meant?

381

IT DIDN'T MATTER how she said it, or who she told. Nobody believed these were not cha, and not a threat.

'Look, the heads come off,' she said to a group at the community centre, who had gathered together for a talk by the mayor entitled:

BREATHING CHA INVASION

'I went on my quest and met my breathing man and turned around and came back, like all sensible people,' the butcher said. 'I had no idea it was also a cha. I thought cha were meant to be friendly creatures! Now it turns out they want to take over our village, chase us out, and kill us all. And they run the universe.'

'Wait,' said Fairly, 'slow down. Where did you hear all that? About cha being bad?'

He couldn't remember.

'So… you all met your own breathing man?' she said.

'They're not. Allowed. In the village,' said the mayor, crossing his arms.

Later that night, in the study, waiting for the chime to ring, her mother said, 'You know, I think you'll come out of this a hero.' Two of the breathing men were in the room too, standing in the corner, their eyes closed. Maybe dreaming. 'You've got a lot to offer,' her mother said. 'You discovered the whole breathing man/ cha conspiracy thing. It went much deeper than I ever expected. We'd heard about the cha statues and such, but this—this makes sense.'

'What sense?'

Her mother said she couldn't explain it. 'I think this is what I've been telling questers on the chime since the beginning, though,' she said. 'You know? I've really known it since I first set out on the horned road.'

'And turned around and came straight back,' said Fairly.

'The world needs to know,' mused her mother.

'My breathing man isn't part of any invasion,' Fairly said.

'How do you know?'

It was the erosion of all she thought she had ever known, had ever discovered. The cracks in the world she had explored. It was all falling apart. Everyone walked around the village gently, quietly, with the shadows of the breathing men upon them, their cha heads firmly back in place. They would not listen to reason and remove the heads. They acted as if the villagers were not speaking at all.

381

SHOULDN'T THERE BE *some solidarity in this experience?* Fairly wondered. They were all being followed by the same man, albeit different copies of him. But the very presence of the men made everyone withdrawn, difficult. Unable to communicate.

Surely there was some way to understand... everything? To find real wisdom, and pass it on to others, no chime needed?

One morning she went down to the river and stood in the water, up to her knees. Her breathing man came along, but stayed on the bank.

'Come on,' she said. 'Get your calves cold. It's good for you.' The feeling was very refreshing, and the sound of trickling water a delight.

He rolled up his cha legs and stepped in. He waded out to draw level with her.

'See?' she said. 'Good, isn't it?' They were together in the morning light, in the grip of the water that flowed past. She remembered something her mother had once said on the chime, to some quester or other: *You can never stand in the same river twice.* She liked it. Refused to reject it on the grounds that her mother had said it.

'Right,' she said. 'Let me try on the head.'

He shook his head.

'Seriously. After all we've been through. I need to try on the head.'

There was a long pause, during which her feet acclimatized to the cold, and went numb. Then the breathing man removed the head and passed it to her.

It was heavy. She clutched it by the horns, and lowered it over her head. Inside, all was dark and still, and stale. The smell of the cha she had known, worked amongst, was strong. She remembered them caring for her, offering her the use of their hot tub, and oinking. It was calm and warm in the head. The world couldn't touch her while the head was in place.

The breathing man was no longer beside her.

She looked at where he had been standing. He was gone. Not gone, exactly. She was aware, on some level, that he had not moved. But she was now in a place where he could not quite be real to her, not quite visible. A great wash of relief came over her. Everything was better inside the head.

381

'No WONDER YOU like wearing it,' she said.

So this was why humans pretended to be cha, worshipped cha, ate cha, traded in cha. This was why they were scared of cha and obsessed with cha. Cha possessed this peace, this unnatural calm, and it was powerful beyond anything she had ever experienced. It was masterful. Any creature that felt this way could rule the world. The universe.

A voice inside her said: *Take it off*.

So there he was—the breathing man, still somehow with her, except only as a quiet sound inside her mind. The head could not erase him utterly. If she listened closely she could hear him breathing away, in, out, in, out. *Take it off*, he said again. There it was, that pleasant voice she knew from the escape pod, deep and songful, and filled with all the emotion his face had never expressed. He was scared, and alone, and naked, and he loved her, and he hated her, and he needed her.

'No,' she told him, 'No. I'm never taking it off ever again.' She waded out of the river. She could barely feel her feet on the walk back to the village, but it didn't matter. She carried her shoes and stubbed her toes on the grass more than once, and it meant nothing to her. Through the eyes of the mask all was good and calm, and the first person she told about her discovery was her mother.

After that, things moved quickly.

The plan was organised on little notes, passed around the village secretly, all written in her mother's hand:

GET THE CHA HEADS. PUT THEM ON.

A date and a time, underneath.

Would everyone do it? Would the breathing men rebel?

Whatever, thought Fairly. It was great inside her head, at least. In fact, the whole thing looked quite comical to her when the mass theft went ahead: the villagers, pouncing, struggling, and then they had cha heads too, and everything was calm and good everywhere.

'Great,' she said. 'All done.' Life would go on. No more to be said. That was all fine, for a while, until everyone realised the children had gone. Not the older ones, but the little ones, who hadn't had breathing men of their own yet.

381

THEY WERE FOUND in a group, huddled together in the nursery, tear-stained and dirty.

'Take off the heads,' they begged. 'We hate them, we hate them.'

But everyone, even their own parents, refused to shed the heads. 'Don't be so silly,' the parents said. 'There's nothing to be afraid of.' The children cried and shrank further into the corner.

Take it off, said the breathing man in her mind. Fairly, feeling annoyance at the situation, decided to play along, for a minute or two. She removed the head and sat with the children.

'It's okay,' she said. 'See? You can try it on, if you like.'

They all shook their heads vehemently. They pointed behind her, behind her parents. Through the window of the nursery, she saw the faces of the breathing men, en masse, still in the village. How forlorn and desperate they looked, as one.

'Get out,' she said to them. 'You're scaring the children.'

But she knew that wasn't what was upsetting the children in the least. The children had been perfectly happy to hang around the breathing men with their masks on before this happened. It was only the parents, the familiar faces, they couldn't stand to lose.

Fairly left the cha head off, tucked it under her arm, and took a walk around the village. The children followed after her.

She saw things the head had kept from her. Other villagers, who had not managed to wrestle free a cha head for themselves, were frightened too. The weak, and the old. She saw the way cha-headed villagers pushed past them, stamped over them, neglecting them, hurting them. The butcher barrelled into her and knocked her over, and the children tried to help her up. 'See?' they said. 'See?' Things were being ruined. The fields were tracked with footprints, destroying the crops. The animals in their pens were hungry.

Fairly stood in the village square, the children gathered around her, and called out, 'Take off the heads! There's work to do and people to care for.'

Everybody with a head on ignored her. If she put her own head back on, then of course they would see her and listen to her. But then she knew she would no longer care about what she could not see.

381

THE BREATHING MEN, the children, and the older, weaker villagers gathered to her. She stood, surrounded by them, and remembered what it felt like to look out at space. To be thousands of miles from this planet and its problems. She had been aware of that slender thread of connection to the idea of home. It had been fragile, but it had never snapped. She realised, then, that her breathing man had kept her tethered. Her emotions for him, about him, his company, the sound of his breath, were important. It meant she was not yet done with the Earth and its ways.

She looked at the people who stood with her, and although all the breathing men looked the same, she knew when she saw her very own breathing man. He pushed forward and held out his hands.

She gave him the cha head, and he carried it, but he did not put it on. Instead he beckoned for her to follow him, for once, for the only time in their relationship, and she walked behind him to the village hall, into the departure lounge, to the dusty sheet under which lurked the chain device.

It had been the start of the quest. Could it be the end? The first and last device, at the top and bottom of the horned road. A reset, maybe. Yes, she desperately wanted a reset.

She pressed the button, and at first it seems that nothing has changed and then I look around the room and see my breathing man is still there, and I see how his breathing is in perfect time with my own and his face is mine, too—not precisely, but yes, undeniably, a copy of my face, altered with long lines and a hard stare. He is the me all these experiences have made. We are older. We are the same.

'Hello,' we say, together, to ourselves, to each other, and we laugh.

The end.

What is that? The final steps of a journey, the culmination of an intention. A moment in which those outside the experience can say, *Enough, we're done.* I don't think I'll ever be done, but I have learned that I won't ever put on a cha head again. That is my intention today, anyway.

381

'WHAT ARE THE cha?' I ask myself, and he says, 'Does it matter?' He says it so fast that I have to think about it for a long time. I sit on the floor of the departure lounge and sort through my memories of cha, my perception of them.

I don't really know anything about them. But I know a lot more about humans.

Here's what I know about humans. I tell it to you for posterity, for all the quest-bound children who might read these words I write, knowing the folly of trying to pass on knowledge, seeing it fail as an exercise on the chime over and over again (but feeling certain about this: what is life if we do not make the effort?).

I know that whatever there is in this world that controls us, it is formed by us.

I know that whatever we create is taken from the world as we walk through it, creating straight and laid-out roads.

I know we don't understand the roads we lay or the forms we create.

Does all this seem circular to you?

Does it seem like the kind of thing my mother would say? Words for the benefit of those outside the experience, not within it? Well, we are all in the experience in one way or another, whether we wear our costume heads or not.

Maybe my future does lie here, in the study over the kitchen, trying to speak my thoughts to the chime, trying to soothe the fears of those who dare to start an adventure and see enemies everywhere rather than dressing up and disguises. And who does rule the world? Is that the real question? The one question I should have attempted to answer all along?

What a waste of time that would be.

I remember a room like a church in space, and the beings that lurked within it. The distance they had attained from the planet had made them feel powerful. How much distance is needed, and how thick must the skin of a mask be?

If the cha rule this world, we are letting them. But I don't think I'm prepared to let them rule me anymore. I want to give up on my own journey along the horned road.

381

I HEAD BACK outside and try to collect the cha heads from the villagers, but they don't see me, and they react violently when they feel pressure on the heads. Even my own mother pushes me away, and screams, 'No!'

'Give it to me,' I say, 'Please. Please.' I touch her arm and she flails, connects with my arm, then rubs her hand as if she has hurt herself. She has no care for me. I can't win this fight. I don't have it in me to hurt her, hold her down, even for her own good. She'll be better off living life her own selfish way.

I retreat to the house and throw a few things in my backpack: the tent, the sleeping bag, a little food. Upstairs, the chime is ringing. I make my way to the study and answer the call, and a voice very like my own, so lost, so young, says, 'Hello?'

'Hello,' I say, 'Hello.' And I let things pour out of me, sentences like:

Don't judge people by their appearances
   and
Try to look behind the masks
   and
Never be afraid of what you imagine the world to be like
   and
Journeys only exist if you move to make them.

That last one sounds familiar. It sounds like something my mother would say.

I stop talking.

The voice is silent for a while, and then it says, 'I don't think I want to do this dance.'

I hang up the chime.

Is this the dance I want to do?

The phone rings again, and I pick it up, and I try again.

And again.

And again.

Everything I say makes no sense. Eventually I let the chime ring. I take my backpack and leave.

The villagers with cha heads are dancing, enjoying themselves, bowling over all the ones without heads, but the ones without are showing signs of organisation. They've picked up spades and forks from the gardening area, and this is about to turn nasty. I shout to them, 'Come with me!' I collect the children from the nursery, and they follow me willingly. The breathing men all come too, and together we make a large group. Enough to start over. I lead the way out through the gate to the horned road.

381

I DON'T TAKE it.

I veer off the road at the first opportunity, over the bracken, tackling the hills, refusing to return to the path.

It's hard going for the little ones, but we manage, helping each other. Even the breathing men take it in turns to carry things.

I start to see sights I've never seen before. Look, look there. Can you see it? Dandelions. I don't think I've ever noticed them before, not like this. How beautiful and wild they are, untidy explosions in the long grass. This—this is the place where we should stop, and rest.

I call a halt and say, 'Here. We'll build here.'

And we start all over again.

A new village, a new way of doing things. Breathing men and children and the weak and the old, and we all get along together, and we make houses and we tend fields and we organise schooling and we hold meetings and we start a singing group. Life is very hard, and often there's not enough to eat, but we persevere. Some people leave and others join, and that's fine. The breathing men start to take on features of their own. They develop personalities. I can't understand why I was so afraid of them, and they seem to have forgotten everything that came before.

We build no roads. Let the outside world do what it does; we have opted out.

It's easy to believe that, until the day comes when a visitor arrives at the gate.

It is the First to Fall.

I recognise him the moment he's shown into my study, although he has aged, yes, and so have I. He is not young anymore, but he is still handsome. Well kept. I greet him, and call him by his name, and he says, 'Wow, nobody's called me that in years! Amazing. It feels weird. I'm Freddie now, actually. I'm here with a gift for you.'

'A gift?' It's years since anybody gave me a gift. Everything I have I've worked hard for, including my children, my beautiful children made with my breathing man, who has a new name of his own: my Bernard.

The First to Fall—Freddie—opens his smart jacket and takes out a handful of cha from his inside pocket.

381

THESE CHA ARE golden, shiny, and each one is exactly alike in size and shape. They are pretty and tempting. Designed to be that way, no doubt. 'Imagine what you could buy with these,' he says. 'Make it an easier life.'

'No thank you,' I tell him, primly, and he laughs.

'You speak for everyone, do you?'

'Do you?'

'I speak for the young,' he says. 'Like the children here, who will one day need to know about such things. Just like we had to learn. Or will you keep them here against their will?'

He lays out the deal. Goods, trades. Wealth I can't imagine, for us all. And in return the village stays as it is, untouched, but the young—only those who would leave anyway, for there is always a choice in this world—can go forth with cha in their pocket. A road will be built to the village. A chain device will be placed in the town hall, and a chime in my study.

'Nearly all of them will come back,' said Freddie. 'It's a small price to pay for immunity.'

'Are you immune?' I ask him. 'Is that what happened to you, the boy I loved, the boy who wanted to see the stars? Where is your breathing man?'

Freddie smiles, his teeth very white, and says, 'I ate him.'

I don't think he is joking.

I tell him I will inform the others, and we will all make a decision together, and I offer him lodgings in the village, which he's pleased to accept. I would like to ask him to drink with me, tell me of his own journey, and how it reached this point. But who can explain such things to another? The more I travel, the more I realise there are no words that make sense, except to say that this is an adventure, and we are all, in our own way, heroes.

I step out and say my hellos to the people I pass. Outside, the dandelions still grow long against the wooden walls.

What makes an old dance into a new one? That's the question I keep asking myself. Just one extra step, and it is a different move to a strange beat.

I must take only one extra step.

Archive: Personal Project PER59683758

Conclusion by Rowena Savalas

4 January 2366

It is not ridiculous to say that agreement can be found in *The Dance of the Horned Road*: not in terms of what we think we know, but in everything that makes us ask the real question at the heart of the document:

What the hell is going on?

I've had a brilliant life. I've had fun. I've changed. How clever I was back at the beginning of this document, how sharp and erudite and innocent, even though I contained all the information ever amassed. The person I was, then, is almost lost to me, unknowable. The fragments that remain are glamorous and strange. There's no way to make sense of them.

Those who say the concept of the quest became irrelevant when we reached a lasting plateau of

273

global peace and prosperity – against all odds,
beyond all expectations, at huge cost to our
humanity – misunderstand what a quest is. I have
been on my own quest for my entire life. I made up
my own rules, and that included telling myself that
I wasn't on a quest in the first place. Trust me to
complicate it. I was seeking to understand the world
now by looking at what had gone before. With a
nod to Dr Magnaman, I now think I was asking the
wrong question. The question is not: *How do I move
forward?* It is: *What do I lose if I don't look back?*

Fairly's journey is confusing, and so is my own.
Here's mine laid out in a form similar to her own,
taken from the very start of the document:

**the start – the rules – the mother – the socialisation
– the breathing man – the message – the boat – the
captain – the Spire – the crew – the wreck – the
breathing man – the land – the bar – the mountains
– the teacher – the dance – the descent – the return
– the job – the teaching – the end – the breathing
man – the dive – the objects – the ageing – the
breathing man – the decision – the document – the
formulation – the theory – the start**

I'm not sure what that proves, other than that nothing
makes sense until you imbue it with your own
meaning.

That is my theory. It lies at the summation of my life, Fairly's journey, and this document. We build our reason for being alive from the experiences we have lived. Not only that: we build it from the lives other people have lived, and it doesn't matter whether they make any sense to us or not. That's why the Age of Curation is the pinnacle of human achievement (so far!); it demands that we mine the Age of Riches, and all previous ages, and define ourselves as better. I've come up with a name for that process. I call it Creative Historical Assembly. I will make a physical object of this document, and gift it to the Unity Spire when my body dies and my digital spirit returns to its home.

One final thought: I worked out why *The Dance of the Horned Road* consists of precisely 381 steps. It came to me soon after the capsizing of the *Commitment to Frivolity*. It's part of the puzzle, and the most basic of codes – possibly one borne of the desperation to communicate something that cannot be said in words or numbers alone.

$$A=1. \ B=2.$$

$$381 = CHA$$

Why?

I don't know.

Maybe it means that we are all part of one huge conspiracy that spans the ages, and this document is the only one that has managed to speak of it, with its message hidden so well within. Maybe cha rule the universe.

Maybe it means I love you.

Maybe it means there is always going to be too much information in this world, and all the tags and compartments we make won't be enough to hold it, shape it, make it manageable. Something will always escape to come roaring up behind us, breathing down our necks.

Maybe it means nothing at all, and we might as well keep dancing down the road without looking back. Instead, look forward, look up! Look at that amazing view, that great creation. That illogical, unreasonable world. It's near, now. It's within our grasp. We have yet to reach perfection, but many think we are close.

This ageing body tires quickly. I think I might go for a sleep. Lately I've been dreaming that old dream of mine: a world without numbers. Formless, orderless. Information without direction, from here to there, from past to future. Continually signposting the way down the endless road.

It doesn't scare me as much as it used to.

Original Metatags:

fantasy – science fiction – journalism –
autobiography – travelogue – quest – geography
– personal – society – satire – conspiracy – space
flight – love – fear – confusion – philosophy – history
– musings – currency – village – town – city – lake
– sea – camping – hotel – camper van – statue –
balloon – rocket – tunnel – sea – land – dance

Appendix A

Taken from *The Backpacker's Buddy: A Guide to Essential Packing for the Committed Rambler.* (Author LGV Michaels, see: VEY96858889.)

Contents of the essential backpack for the seasoned traveller:

1 x small instapak tent
1 x sleeping bag/compression sack
1 x mallet
24 x tent pegs
1 x water canteen (762 ml min)
40 x water purifying tablets
1 x collapsible stove
1 x solar torch
1 x folding pot
30 x food pouches
30 x small energy bars

30 x daily vitamins

1 x knife

1 x fork

1 x spoon

1 x plate

1 x bowl

1 x mug

1 x teatowel

1 x compass

75 x matches in waterproof box

2 x replacement shoelaces

3 x lightweight quick dry underwear

3 x lightweight tee shirts

2 x sturdy trousers

4 x socks

1 x sunscreen

10 x blister plasters

10 x regular plasters

1 x antiseptic spray

1 x insect repellent

16 x antihistamine tablets

16 x paracetamol/NSAID tablets

1 x sling

1 x safety scissors

1 x needle

1 x spool of thread

1 x lightweight towel

1 x body wash/shampoo bar
30 x refuse sacks
30 x sanitary towels (or equivalent sanitary products)
1 x Swiss army knife/reliable make of penknife
1 x spool of string

ACKNOWLEDGEMENTS

THE WORLD WAS a really strange, locked-down place when I first started writing *Three Eight One*, and I had no idea what was going on for a while. First readers Tim Stretton, George Sandison, and Christopher Priest: you made it a much better book and helped me focus on the task at hand. I'm incredibly grateful for your insights and encouragements.

To my agent Max Edwards, at Aevitas Creative Management—thank you so much for your commitment and energy. The cover is the work of the talented Dominic Forbes. And I'm delighted that this book has been published with such care and creativity by Solaris Books. Thanks to David Thomas Moore, Jess Gofton, Dagna Dlubak and Chiara Mestieri.

Finally, a massive truckload of thanks to everyone who listened to me moan about the strangeness of the world while writing this book. Sorry in particular to Jim Ovey, Nick and Nicola Porecki, and my amazing, patient family. Let's keep dancing.

ABOUT THE AUTHOR

Aliya Whiteley is one of the most exciting talents in the UK. She is the author of seven books of speculative fiction, and has been shortlisted for the Arthur C. Clarke Award, the Shirley Jackson Award and the Otherwise Award. She lives in Sussex with her husband and daughter.

🌐 aliyawhiteley.uk

FIND US ONLINE!

www.rebellionpublishing.com

/solarisbooks /solarisbks /solarisbooks

SIGN UP TO OUR NEWSLETTER!

rebellionpublishing.com/newsletter

YOUR REVIEWS MATTER!

Enjoy this book? Got something to say?

Leave a review on Amazon, GoodReads or with your favourite bookseller and let the world know!

Arthur C. Clarke Award Nominated Author

ALIYA WHITELEY

THE BEAUTY

TENTH ANNIVERSARY EDITION

⊙ SOLARISBOOKS.COM